ANTONIO

Also by BEATRIZ BRACHER
from New Directions

•

I Didn't Talk

Beatriz Bracher

ANTONIO

translated from the Portuguese
by Adam Morris

A NEW DIRECTIONS
PAPERBOOK ORIGINAL

Originally published in Brazil as *Antônio* by Editora 34.
Rights to this edition negotiated via literary agent Patricia Seibel
in association with Agência Riff.

Manufactured in the United States of America
First published as a New Directions Paperbook (NDP1492) in 2021
Design by Erik Rieselbach

Library of Congress Cataloging-in-Publication Data
Names: Bracher, Beatriz, author. | Morris, Adam J., translator.
Title: Antonio / Beatriz Bracher ; translated from the Portuguese by Adam Morris.
Other titles: Antonio. English
Description: New York : New Directions Publishing Corporation, 2021. |
Originally published in Brazil as Antônio by Editora 34.
Identifiers: LCCN 2020044028 | ISBN 9780811227384 (paperback) |
ISBN 9780811227391 (ebook)
Classification: LCC PQ9698.412.R33 A5813 2021 | DDC 869.3/5—dc23
LC record available at https://lccn.loc.gov/2020044028

2 4 6 8 10 9 7 5 3 1

New Directions Books are published for James Laughlin
by New Directions Publishing Corporation
80 Eighth Avenue, New York 10011

ANTONIO

Raul

Whenever anyone asked how many siblings he had, Teo would say, "There are five of us, but one died." If this confused whoever asked, Teo would only shake his head and say: "I never met him. He was the eldest and died when he was a baby." Teo and I were classmates since elementary school. I became a friend of the family and spent a lot of time over at their place. When we were young, it was a cheerful house—much different than the one you got to know. Aside from earning whatever she could teaching classes at the high school and then the university, your grandma Bel took care of everything. She made sure the chaos never totally overwhelmed them. Xavier was an editor, writer, journalist, and dramaturge, so I figure their day-to-day expenses were paid by Bel's work and, from what I could gather, the remains of an inheritance. They lived in Butantã, in a house that belonged to Xavier's father—your great-grandfather, the doctor. When I was a kid, there weren't many houses on that street. Theirs must have been one of the first. You went there when you were very little—I don't know if you'd remember. There was a yard with trees, and sunny rooms with high ceilings. The broken furniture never got fixed; it eventually just disappeared. The emptiness expanded, so the interior of the house seemed to grow as the years went by. We'd build cities and ranches on the parquet floors, and they'd stay there for months without bothering anyone. When the wooden wedges in the floor started to come loose, they became walls and bridges, and the tar and sawdust underneath transformed into patches of rocky terrain. Then came the days of balsa planes and plastic monsters, the constant smell of glue and ink. The button soccer board must have stayed there until the house was demolished. Later on there were all those cushions where we'd spend hours lounging and talking, playing guitar, watching TV without the sound, and eating crackers and cream cheese. Nadia Comaneci in the '76 Olympics and Sonia Braga in *Dancing Days*. The walls covered in newspaper clippings, the shelves stuffed with books and binders, and photos Scotch-taped to the paint. It was sort of like a bunker, or maybe the reverse: we had sunlight, air, books, TV, the guitar, and Graça's white cake. In the event a nuclear war broke out, we could've survived there for years.

I never saw a single picture of this dead brother, and the baby boy's death didn't seem to weigh on the family. Bel liked to tell stories about her kids when they were little, but she never talked about him. So I started to think that maybe it was just a gothic invention of your father's. One day, sometime near the end of that era of cushions and weed, I asked him about that brother. Your father stopped strumming the guitar, became very serious, and said:

"Up until last week even I didn't really know anything about it either. I'd heard my dad tell people the same thing: I have five children, but one of them died. And so I started saying it, too: there's five of us, but one died. I knew that this other son of his was born before he married my mom—the result of a fling in his youth. I thought the phrase had a heroic ring to it for those of us who survived. And something supernatural, too, because he always said *I have* and not *I had*, suggesting that all five of us remained with him in the present. Then a week ago I was on the phone with Helinho and I laughed and said, there are five of us, but one's dead. I think it had something to do with Rafa, who swore he wouldn't come play button soccer with the rest of us until he passed his college entrance exam. My father was nearby and overheard me. He asked me why I was making light of such a serious subject. You know my father— you know how he is when he gets serious."

I don't know if you remember your grandfather, but he adored you. Xavier was a special person. He could turn anything into a gag or a joke, including his own failures. He was always devising some new way of making money from theater or literature. One time he came up with the idea of printing cheap books and selling them at newspaper stands and distributing them to street vendors. Books with plenty of action and sex, sexy women on the covers and "metaphysical messages between the lines." They even sold pretty well: they were funny and not at all metaphysical. But Xavier always figured out a way to blow his investments and end up owing even more than he did before he started. He also went through a period of trying to do this improvisational musical-dance-theater-circus thing. He'd place announcements in the newspaper for a theater class that was open to anyone but professional actors. He didn't believe in acting workshops; he preferred magic and pirouettes, makeup, rags, feathers—and always music. Trumpeting fanfare, cello solos, Spanish guitar, samba sung a cappella, the dry wooden taps of indigenous music. He'd gather a bunch of people in the garage and put on a traveling show—an andante performance in several movements connected by an invisible plot. In the seventies he managed to put on a few of these shows. They'd start in the street at six in the evening, marching by the crowded bus stops and the bustling doorways of factories during the evening shift change. The spectators were part of the show, but they only realized after it had gone by. I saw one of those shows, in which Teo was one of

5

the musicians. It was pretty amazing: sort of like a breeze, or a dream. Even though they were all done up with costumes and props for vaudeville and the circus, the performance was soft and sweet, almost like a landscape. It was the complete opposite of the Theater of the Oppressed: it was a theater of the irrepressible. It eased some of the tension in the streets and lightened the hearts of people who got to see it. Nobody made any money off it, and your grandfather invariably lost much of his own. That was why he kept working as a journalist and art critic for several newspapers and magazines. He worked like a dog and lived for leisure—always ready with a bon mot and making the kind of scenes that embarrassed his children, especially as we all got older.

That's why when he became serious—really serious, not fanatic or megalomaniacal, but serious—it was something that scared us. He changed colors, as though his blood had started running the other way through his veins. His eyes got dark and his saliva thickened. We listened quietly and all felt the urge to get up and go when he, always so articulate, started stuttering.

"So then," Teo continued, "he told me that he, my father, would always be—before all else—the father of this dead boy, his son Benjamim dos Santos Kremz." That's right: the same name as yours. Now hold on, listen: I remember everything I ever knew about it, but I never knew that much. I have an unbearably good memory—that's why I'm so good at my job, with all those announcements, jingles, slogans. I'm a professional plagiarist, which is also how I knew your name was going to be the same as that dead brother's, the full name on the death certificate I just showed you. At the time it didn't occur to me that your mother could be the same one—Santos is such a common name. The amazing thing is that what disturbed you just now when you saw the certificates, those papers that Leonor found and wanted you to see—the whole twisted thing is true, it seems. That is, your mother, Elenir, was married to your grandfather and had a child by him, a child who then died—the first Benjamim. An insanity that I only just now learned about—Leonor told me before she left. A truly crazy thing. For your grandfather, Elenir was Lili, and to your father she was Leninha.

Starting again from the beginning will help you understand at least part of this tangled knot. All that business about "There are five of us" happened just before he went to Minas. Your father spoke in hushed tones, he was so excited. "He said he'd never told me about Benjamim because it wasn't just a story, like one of his theater projects, or the make-believe of children—it wasn't just the tribulations of new parents. No, it was the story of his rebirth, the birth of Xavier the adult, the real Xavier, a delivery in which Xavier the boy had to die." I didn't understand, and said so. I saw that Teo was still struggling with it himself. "I didn't really understand either, and my father seemed to regret that he'd started telling me. I asked how old my brother was when he died. He got emotional when he heard me call his son my brother—his eyes welled up and I felt ashamed. He said that he was less than a month old, that his mother was very young, that it was a difficult birth, and that they'd used forceps and messed up and crushed the baby's head. He ended up with birth defects and died in the first month. The whole thing was still very difficult for him." We sat there in silence. Teo wasn't one to get emotional. On the contrary, he looked down on sentimentality. I was the sensitive one, and I often suffered the brunt of his sarcasm. He demanded so much from himself, and he was always on guard against going soft. But he needed to unload on someone about that conversation with Xavier. He was searching for the right words.

"You know, it was like my father was telling me a secret I already knew. He was lifting the veil from something I didn't recognize, but always knew existed. He spoke about his love for other people, about his ability to get close, really close, to other people. Only this time he wasn't talking about his theater or one of his classes, but real life. He was talking about his feelings and the sense of direction that Benjamim's birth and death had given him. He told me the mother of this brother of mine was a special woman, and after everything that happened he couldn't stay at his desk at the firm, he needed to start over. He tried to go on, stuttering more through each sentence—but I had to get out of there, I had to get away from him. The way he was talking made me feel like I had something to do with the death of his son—it was something half-crazy. Something saccharine and cloying. In the heat of the moment I got angry—I'm not sure why. If this was so important, why hadn't he told me about it before? And obviously it was important, a brother who'd died, it was something I'd never seriously considered. Later I got sad, as though this Benjamim had just died a few days beforehand. I don't know—it was like we'd taken his place, without anybody ever saying his name in our home. But in my father's heart he loomed larger than us all. It's very strange. He'll always be the eldest and the baby—dead, but alive whenever my father looks at any of us, or at anyone else."

And Benjamim, let me tell you, it really *was* strange, especially in that house, the way a story like that wasn't already known to everyone, endlessly commented and dissected, sucked down to the bone. Everyone and everything in that family required commentary, nobody was exempt. I think it was part of the times we were living in—the belief that we had the obligation to eliminate taboos, that the spoken word possessed that sort of power. In the Kremz household, everyone had to have an opinion. Sometimes a disagreement would end in a shouting match; other times it was resolved by consulting the encyclopedia, dictionaries, books—or quite often, by Xavier's dissatisfying conclusion that nobody was getting anywhere, that they were all too tired to go on. Your aunts Flora and Leonor were the two most modern girls I knew. I think it was the first house where boyfriends and girlfriends were allowed to spend the night together, and we could smoke whatever we wanted without a fuss. There was a real violence of ideas, an obligation to be alert to what was happening in the world, to submit everything to rubrics of analysis, curiosity, and taste. With that burden of culture and liberalism, I preferred to remain just an add-on to the family, and later return to my private and well-furnished house.

Teo was the youngest. Flora was already working by then; Henrique and Leonor were in college. And by the time he sat for entrance exams that year, Teo still had no idea what we wanted to do. Passing the exam wasn't the problem. It wasn't as hard back then as it is now, and everyone in that family was practically a genius. The real difficulty was choosing a career. He was the sharpest of our set: he wrote, drew, played, composed. He was a math whiz ever since grade school, always a few levels ahead of everyone else. Everything came so easily to him. Maybe that was why he hesitated—and actually, in his senior year Teo began to force himself to be a bad student. After that conversation with his father, it seemed like he put some things together in his head—something clicked with one of his preconceived notions, and he decided he didn't want to go to college. He was sick of São Paulo and wanted to take a break, he wanted to travel, to see the *sertão*—things that don't make any sense today, but which, back then, were still in the realm of possibilities.

Isabel

No, Benjamim, I don't think your father went to the *sertão* to find your mother. That was a coincidence. I never met Elenir, but I imagine she was beautiful and had the sort of charm that drew her to the Kremz family. And no, I don't think Teodoro intended to pay for his father's suffering, as though it were a sin that demanded his atonement—not least because there was no sin in the first place. Whenever Xavier spoke about the year he spent with Elenir, it was with the tone of someone describing a lost love affair. In fact, I'm not really sure why they went their separate ways. Knowing Xavier, I'm sure he didn't abandon her. He never told this part of the story, at least not to me. I said that he never abandoned her because he fought with his parents, left home, and refused anyone's help—all so he could be with her. Elenir was a simple girl living in São Paulo, away from her parents. I think she would've been about fifteen at the time. A lot of his friends started keeping their distance. I know this because Haroldo told me their affair became the talk of São Paulo. Haroldo was his classmate at São Francisco, the law school, and was one of the few who stuck by him. I believe he knew your mother well. Just think: these days, a rich kid who gets a poor girl pregnant would be totally ostracized if he didn't take responsibility for the child and help pay for child support. Back then it was the exact opposite. The boy's family and even some of his friends would tell him the girl should "figure something out," as they used to say. Or they'd send her back to wherever she came from with a little bit of money. And just like that, nobody ever mentions it again. Xavier was in love with your mother—it wasn't a simple matter of taking responsibility . That was the story he told.

I think it was Elenir who jumped ship, because she couldn't tolerate Xavier's grief. Your grandfather was always a bit manic—even his joys were hard to contain. It's not easy to tolerate feelings like that. She was so young, a simple girl, an orphan. You see, Benjamim, you were also born motherless, but you had your father and then you had me. You were born into a family. Your father, in spite of it all … It wouldn't be fair to say that he abandoned you. He abandoned himself—I think by now you're able to tell the difference. Maybe for a son it's still something unforgivable. But when you get to be my age, trapped in a hospital room and knocking on purgatory's door, maybe you'll be able to understand what happened. With Elenir, I can only guess. It's likely that at fifteen she thought she'd found a husband and a family. And I'm almost certain Xavier wanted the same thing. I realize this is completely banal, but in Elenir he sought the family he'd never really had. Your grandfather's mother was a proper lady, everything absolutely comme il faut. Intelligent, generous, elegant, self-sufficient. Your great-grandfather was a renowned scientist, a celebrated public health advocate, a great benefactor of hospitals. He had all of humanity to look after. Yes, I think Xavier might just have experienced a rebirth after that affair with Elenir, after the death of that poor child. It's a realistic outcome of his line of thinking, and I'm not surprised you got the idea from Raul's rather fantastic imagination. That poor child. The bad luck of having to be a father to his own parents, forcing them to be reborn—it was too much for a such a small being to bear.

We never knew you were Elenir's son. When you were born and your mother died, Teodoro never told us anything. He only said your mother was called Leninha and that she worked in the ward where he was hospitalized after coming down with malaria—or whatever was giving him those fevers and deliriums. I never knew he was sick—in fact, I didn't even know where he was. He'd write or call from time to time, telling us he was retracing Guimarães Rosa's path through the backlands, perfecting his guitar skills. That was just in the beginning. After a while he didn't call anymore, and only wrote a few letters, always from different places. In the first letters he seemed excited about his new life. He'd say he was always reminded of Vanda, their nanny, that wherever he was living people told the same stories he'd known ever since he was little. They sang the same lullabies. In the summer of that first year, Raul went out to see him. He said Teodoro was doing well, he was happy, had short hair, and spoke with a Minas accent about making plans to settle down. I never imagined that he referred to having a family. He was only eighteen. Raul didn't tell us anything about the accident on the boat, or about Teodoro's disappearance.

When Teo left São Paulo he was already pretty lost. I thought it would do him good to travel, to find his way forward. Teodoro was always the one most different from his father. Ever since he was little he was neat and orderly. He reminded me when to take him to school, when to give him his medicine and cut his nails. I think that, because he was the baby of the family, it was his way of surviving. At fifteen or sixteen he started giving private tutoring lessons and making his own money. We could have helped him out, but he never asked. He'd say he was doing just fine, picking up work in the towns where he stayed, that he still had his savings. It's possible that he wasn't eating well, but that wasn't something I could discern from his letters or calls. I was never too concerned about nutrition or health when it came to my kids. We had those kind of ideas about how to raise them, and even after everything that's happened, I still believe that freedom is the most fundamental aspect of an individual's self-formation, including the freedom to die. Without that risk we're not masters, only slaves. I raised my children this way, you know that, Benjamim. I'd like to think your mother was also a free person, and maybe you can hold on to that thought, instead of clinging to fear and rage.

Anyway, back to the story: Teodoro got excited by music, and by the people he met. In that way he resembled Xavier. He didn't have the same missionary fervor—no, he was always the one transformed. You're now older than your father was when you were born. Today everything is different. It's hard to explain. I still don't really know whether we were fools, or if all of you, today, are lazy and boring and weak. We thought the world would be transformed and that we would be the catalysts for that transformation. And today it makes us seem like fools. Whatever you make of all this, it's important for you to remember the idiosyncratic ideals of those days. Otherwise you'll never understand what I'm trying to tell you.

Teodoro, although he was the youngest, was the most mature of my children. I trusted him, I never feared for his future. If he thought he was capable of wandering through the *sertão*, then that was what he had to do. And if your mother had survived, I don't know why she wouldn't have been the right woman for him. You're young, you travel, you find the love of your life, you shack up, have a kid, and that's the end of it. That's what life is, the best parts of it anyway. You're living through it now, so maybe you know what I mean. Your wife is pregnant, you're still in love, you're thinking about what to name your child, already imagining his face. You're going to call him Antonio? Yes, I do like it. It's serious but unassuming. You say that your mother was much older, over forty, but so what? They loved each other, didn't they? Teodoro's madness came later. It wasn't madness that drove him to your mother—that I won't believe. Xavier was a bit abnormal, too, but with me he managed to live a productive life, raise four children, bring joy to many people.

Xavier was always like a child, his whole life. Remember when you'd come to spend vacations here, when you were three or four years old? He already had advanced emphysema and was nearing his painful end. We had to sell the house. We tried all kinds of expensive treatments, but nothing worked. I think that was why your dad decided to bring you: he wanted his father to know his grandson. He knew it would make him happy. You were a joy to Xavier, a shining sun—a sunset. When he saw you, when he heard your voice, the color would rise back into his ashen face. By this point, Henrique's Fábio had already been born. But to your grandfather, you were always different from the other grandchildren. The last time you came for the holidays you must've been about four. It was an especially dry July and Xavier no longer had the energy for long walks. One day you went to the zoo with your father and your cousin, and Xavier insisted on going along. The truth is that he felt better when you were near. It was an illusion, a desire to have enough life left in him to share it with you. He came back exhausted from all the walking, but happy as a clam. I could tell something wasn't right. I asked Teo to leave and take you away with him—your grandfather wasn't going to last much longer. A week later he died, and Teodoro didn't come to the funeral.

Maybe Xavier figured out who you were. And then died in peace. I don't think so. No. This isn't a beautifully intricate novel in which your mother is the hero and I'm the character who picks up the pieces of her broken love. No. Benjamim, the story of our lives still isn't finished, and it never will be. Creating this space for your mother, this narrative for your father and your grandfather, as though nothing had transpired between one Benjamim and the next, or as thought it had only been an echo, a gap, a void between a lost love and its reencounter—that's rather poor. Look, Benjamim, it makes sense, but only a little. We're not literature, my dear. We're love and sperm, blood, laughter, hatred, death and illness, phlegm and farts, baths, medicine, doctors, schools, tests, guitar, English, swimming, ballet, maids, nannies, fingernail clippings, toothbrushes, cuts, Mercurochrome, lice, chicken pox, potassium permanganate, tears, birthday candles, holidays, beaches, horses, tumbles, joys, work, salaries, inheritance, time, and so much more that comes between one encounter and the next. This is what you're made of, too, and it's much more complicated than a love story.

Haroldo

It was in '49, no, '50—my last year at college. Your grand-father was the top student in our class at São Francisco, president of the law school senate. He was a charismatic politician, and the class poet. He had philosophical ambitions. He was already making overtures to your grandmother. Isabel Belmiro was a *must*: a modern girl who'd read everything and held advanced views, who went to bars with boys but came from a good family. It isn't true that she never met Elenir. She met her once, but gave her the Irish goodbye. Maybe she didn't want to get to know her—that would be in keeping with my dear friend's refinement. The thing is that Xavier was passionate, his whole life through. He managed to be passionate about certain street corners, the side of a building, the way an elderly person's earlobe sagged. He was strange like that—he always was. Isabel was exuberant. She dominated her surroundings with her foxy mannerisms and that air of being a French intellectual. She was the most popular girl in the neighborhood. Not in the way you're thinking, but naturally that was part of her charm, too. She wasn't a flirt, but generous and aloof. She's still the same, nothing's changed. She's more somber now, of course—75 years aren't nothing—but she still maintains the independent spirit she cherished in those days.

So you want to know about Elenir. Isabel called and told me everything—I had no idea. How about it, my boy? Seems like you're the son of Elenir and Xavier's crazy son. The same Elenir who brought my friend to his knees back in 1950. What year were you born? In '79 … yes, she would have been about fifteen going on sixteen when she met Xavier. I met Teodoro, your father, when he was still a kid, and again later, after he'd gone insane. He was eaten away by his illness and slowly killing my dear friend Isabel.

To be honest, I didn't spend much time with Isabel and Xavier after they got married. Life took us in different directions. After the thing with Elenir, Xavier completely changed course. A chasm opened between us. We'd been very close friends, so we still got together pretty often. But our families never really connected. I continued studying law, became a lawyer, and then a professor in the law school. I have my practice, I married Fernanda, and we raised a far more conventional family than Xavier and Isabel did. Even so, we remained friends until he died. I remember one time when I visited the old house, he'd had some kind of episode and was recovering in bed. I think this was before you were born. He missed his son. He'd insist that he didn't, saying that everyone had to accept his own lot. But it was obvious he missed him. After all, he was a stay-at-home dad, very much a family man. I don't think he took it well when the house started emptying out. During that visit he showed me a portrait of Teodoro. He had the same face as his father's when we were in college together. The same shoulders, the same gaze and skin tone—everything the same. It must have given your mother quite a fright.

Elenir was an intelligent creature, tall and thin. She looked like a doll. I remember her well. She had smooth black hair, long and thick like a girl's, and dark olive-toned skin with green, almond-shaped eyes. She must've had some Indian blood. Everything made sharp angles: her elbows, her knees, her chin. She wasn't the kind of beauty who attracts attention, but later you'd notice certain things and it would be hard to take your eyes off her. With Xavier it was love at first sight. With Xavier everything was always like that, but she didn't see things that way. Elenir was intelligent, but she wasn't from here. I'm not even sure what planet she was from. At fifteen she was already studying science, and she was very quick to reason through the most complex problems. But she always seemed a bit dense in terms of social grace. I don't mean that she had some kind of country-girl innocence or modesty, no, nothing like that. She wasn't shy—but serious in a way that seemed strange for a woman.

Xavier was finishing the law program, interning with a good firm on Riachuelo. He was a professional man, and an eye-catching one at that. Just think of what your father used to look like, you'll get the idea. He made quite an impression on the ladies. But your grandfather wasn't a flirt. Of course, we both had a lot of girls—but that was another matter. What I mean is that he was a respectful young man. He only liked to play around a bit. If he had the opportunity, he'd steal a kiss on the cheek, a silly caress, nothing serious. Elenir didn't understand. So you know what happened? It's hard to talk about this with you. First of all, you're her son. But the other thing is that whenever I tell a younger man about anything that happened in my youth, it feels like I always have to make excuses—for who knows what. I don't know what kind of prudes we gave birth to. It's one thing for younger women to be this way, but with my grandsons it's the same litany. Nobody sleeps with the maid anymore, with the laundress's daughter, or with the pretty young teachers. It all seems horribly abject to your generation, a pretentious bunch of dandies. It's easy ass—yes, I'm being crude, but it's true. Today you just pity the girl who doesn't go to bed with her first boyfriend. Or not even her boyfriend. Just take a look around at this club: look at how the girls strut around. Look at their clothes: it's complete provocation. And they give it up, it doesn't have to be a boyfriend. Not to an old man like me, obviously, it's not that simple, but anyway you know what I mean. In Rio it must be even easier. But it wasn't like that back then, and like I was saying, it was more fun.

You're Elenir's son, but you're a Kremz, a man, not a little boy. If you came looking for me it's because you want to hear what I have to say. Anyway what happened wasn't anything like that. Your mother wasn't a laundress or a maid. Like I said, she came from another planet. Have you met any grandparents or aunts and uncles from her side? No, exactly, it's just like I said. I think Elenir's father was from the interior. So it's likely that after her mother died, she ended up here through some kind of charity, studying with nuns at a school for poor girls. She was lively and intelligent, a survivor. And when Xavier met her, she had plans to go to medical school. Look, it's like I was telling you: she was a completely different sort of girl. She didn't want anything to do with teaching or nursing or literature—no. She wanted to be a doctor. She lived in a boardinghouse and worked part time as a waitress in the café at the office where your grandfather was doing his internship. I don't know how the whole thing started. I can easily imagine Xavier flirting with the girl, bringing her candy one day, a pretty little bow the next. I can picture the two of them going for coffee after work. I know that she liked to read and that he brought her books of poetry. Maybe they read poetry together. It happened the way it always happens, there was nothing mysterious about it. I don't know what Xavier's intentions were. He wasn't a fool, and I don't think he ever meant to take things very far. He was bewitched, it's true, but I don't think he ever intended to introduce Elenir to his friends. I knew about their affair, which wasn't an affair, really, just a bachelor's fling. Since we were friends I'd sometimes go to his office to chat, and that's when I started to see what was happening. I was a real bastard, and he knew it. We told each other everything. As soon as I met the girl, I sort of brushed her off. Xavier's reaction gave him away—I realized what was happening, and saw the whole thing was a lot more serious than even he imagined.

What I know is that he stopped going out so often with his friends, he stopped being a regular at his usual haunts. He disappeared from the student center, saying he had to study for finals and didn't have time for anything else. He'd managed to get hired as a clerk at the law office and was tied down with work. I knew that it wasn't that simple. Like I said, Xavier was always a little strange. His closest friends could all tell that something was up—it wasn't just his eccentricity. We saw his mood swings: one morning he'd go around kissing the whole law school on the cheek, laughing at everything, and then later that afternoon he'd get into such an ugly fight he'd end up leaving with a bloody nose. After a while he started to crack. He was barely sleeping, saying it was due to work. But the truth is that he'd decided to get married and was saving up the money to do it.

One night I managed to corner him and we ended up talking all night. We drank a lot, but I remember the words he used. He realized he was getting into something crazy, he saw no other way out, he didn't want a way out. The problem was some kind of cross between a grandiose, chimerical sense of duty and a sick jealousy. And with sadness I realized that the trigger for both of these pathological sentiments had to do with my flippant attitude the very first time I saw Elenir. I spoke to her in the same way that he probably would've done many times before—the way future lawyers talk to pretty waitresses. Seeing himself, and moreover, seeing Elenir, through my eyes—it mortified him. And this isn't just me talking: he told me so himself. He said it was in that moment that he saw the mistake he was making. He realized he was as good as dead if he persisted in his error. That's the kind of thing Xavier would say—he was rather grandiloquent. We all were, it was part of our juvenile cynicism. In this case, however, Elenir had castrated my friend's cynicism. He became a child in her hands, and at the same time, a ferocious, terrible man capable of protecting his beloved from social disdain and the coveting lust of other males.

They married in a little chapel kept by nuns. I don't think they could've gotten a civil ceremony because she was a minor and there was no one legally empowered to emancipate her. What was important to Xavier was that he prove his honor, the honor of his love. I don't know who he had to prove it to. And maybe I'm wrong. But at the time, that was how I saw it. After they were married and moved into that neighborhood where they remained for nearly a year, I could tell they were happy. Maybe too happy. I guess the surest thing you could say was that he got married because he was really in love, something even more complicated than class or honor. But as for her—I really have no idea.

The pregnancy prevented Elenir from continuing with her studies. I don't know if she was already pregnant when thy married, but that was what people said—that it was the real reason they got married. People said she should go back to her village so she could give birth the same way her mother had given birth to her—terrible things like that, or worse. I'm not sure if she was pregnant. I think Xavier would have married her either way. Their house was adorable, and what little furniture they had was simple. Xavier broke things off with his parents and earned his own living with his salary as a junior attorney. Elenir had good taste and was a clever girl, resourceful in the ways that nuns taught girls to be. She could make do with very little. She sewed curtains with colorful embroidery, hand-fashioned lighting fixtures out of wires and fabric, and painted landscapes right onto the walls. In the room meant for the baby, she painted birds on the walls and stars on the ceiling. She was talented all right. I think it was her first real home, and she seemed happy. Not like a little bourgeois housewife who had her life figured out. No, she was more like a girl on holiday, amusing herself by spoiling her husband and building a nest. She said those days were a vacation for her, and that after her son was born, she'd resume her studies and become a doctor—as though she needed to justify that period of undeserved happiness. Xavier was dazed, a complete fool. At the office he had more energy than ever, but at the stroke of five he dropped everything and rushed home to his Lili. I visited them a few times, always without invitation. I admit I was morbidly fascinated with them—I wanted to know how the whole thing would end. I don't know why, but it was obvious to me that it wouldn't last very long. The joy, the new pregnancy, and what was probably a lot of sex—it had made Elenir more seductive than ever. As she bloomed and plumped, Xavier started pushing away the few friends who had remained by his side. It wasn't just a question of jealousy anymore, but a total disinterest in anything that didn't have to do with Elenir. There wasn't space for anyone else in that house.

After the child was born there were days in the hospital, those days back and forth between home and the hospital. At Benjamim's burial, Elenir was thin again, but it was no longer a girlish slenderness. She was a serious woman, closed and complete. She looked like a bent piece of wood. She didn't cry. She received each condolence with correct politeness. I never saw her again. Xavier was the total opposite: he was in pieces, a crumpled heap of a man. He locked himself alone in the house and wouldn't open up for anybody. He took a knife to all the linens, the curtains, the chandeliers. He ripped the stuffing out of all the upholstery in the house, and then tore it apart with his teeth. He scraped Elenir's landscapes and birds from the walls with his fingernails. His hands bled. He scrawled out his delusions and nightmares on the walls, on shreds of bedsheets, in notebooks and books, whatever he had in front of him. I managed to gain entry to that hell three times. The last time, I brought a team of nurses, to drag my friend out of there and take him to a sanitorium. That house, after all that, was the only lugubrious place I've seen in my life. Afterward, I retired the use of that word for any other situation.

Raul

Carmem gets up early to take the kids to school and starts work right after that. She can't stay awake this late. If you stay in São Paulo, we could get lunch over the weekend. She wants to see you, and I want you to meet my kids. When I told her about our conversations, I remembered a few things, and she reminded me of some others. About when we were up in Minas, on the steamboat, in Petrolina, when we were all on the cusp of adulthood. I only wanted to tell you about the good times, or about the end—about the Teo your face and gestures remind me of. But that's not what you ... it wasn't like that, it wasn't *only* like that. There's the middle part, too.

It's hard—hard for me, and it's going to be hard for you, too, I think, but that's how it was, right? You lived through the worst of it, you were by his side, weren't you? Anyway, what I can help you with is the part you didn't live through, or rather, the parts I saw from the other side, at a different age, with different ghosts haunting me, a different vantage point. So that I don't skip over anything, it's better if I go in order, day by day.

Your father had been away from São Paulo for nearly a year, and when we met up in Minas, I barely recognized him. He was extremely sunburnt, thin, and had short hair. He was only wearing swim trunks and flip flops. He looked like one of the local boys. We'd planned to take the steamboat up the São Francisco river with a group of friends, all the way up to Petrolina, in Pernambuco. I arrived in the little town of Jequitinhonha, where he was living at the time, ten days before the trip was supposed to begin. It was only later that he went to live in Cipó—I think it was in search of a more disciplined life than the one he was leading there, in that open, unfenced wilderness. I stayed with the family he was living with. It was a little village with just two streets, a dirt plaza, and fields of grass with houses scattered around it. We slept on straw mats. We went hiking and swimming in the river, and sometimes danced forró at night with some of the girls he'd met. Your father helped out when there was work to be done. He learned how to build adobe walls and whitewash them. He earned enough money for food, sometimes a little more. He was thin and happy. An unwavering self-absorption. It was hard for me to follow along.

It was awesome to swim in the river, sit smoking in silence, warm ourselves by the fire, and drink pinga while listening to Teo play his guitar until dawn. And there were those nocturnal noises, learning to identify every creature by its sound. Watching life go by more slowly, under that incredible sky. We felt everything more acutely. That macro lens that smoking sometimes gives you—out there, it felt like something in the air. Helping to castrate a horse, scoop larvae out from under a cow's hide, carrying water from the river. Doing everything ourselves, by hand. I was in that atmosphere, but not of it.

Teo and I had done everything together up to that point. We didn't need to speak to understand each other. And in spite of that we spoke quite a bit—talking for hours, days, and years on end. We spent so many afternoons and late nights together, always talking, talking. Today I wouldn't be able to do it—I don't know how we came up with so many things to discuss. Now I have a better understanding of what was going with Teo. During that time in the middle of Minas, I was disoriented, and it irritated me. He'd always been something of an example for me—we were reflections of one another. What I mean is that each of us measured himself against the other. I was always a little more bold about sticking my nose into things, I didn't let things get complicated. He was more articulate and suave, he had a way with words. He could go deeper than I ever could. We complemented one another. Everything clicked, came together. But in Minas it was different. Maybe it was because I'd started college, had begun to read and discover new things—literary theory, philosophy, manifestoes—I was exposed to new voices, ancient authors from a hundred, two hundred, twenty-five hundred years ago, and all these acquisitions and substitutions were unstable and subject to constant reorganization. I was discovering my infinite and liberating ignorance, which displaced my adolescent certainties. For the first time, my studies truly interested me, challenged me—the world was new and interesting in a completely different way. The old-fashioned boundaries of law and tradition, whether innovative or inherited—they lost all meaning. And Teo seemed to be on the other side of a different boundary. I wanted to tell him about life at the university, about the books I was reading, about Carmem, that I'd started dating her and he still hadn't met her, about the different paths our friends were starting down, about the parties he'd missed. But he wasn't interested.

After a few days I calmed down. I forgot about the speed of life in São Paulo and managed to slip into the rhythm of the place. The people there were amazing, they liked me as Teo's friend—they thought my long hair was funny. Teo told me about what it was like to live there, about the worldview that the people had, about their old way of producing and dividing things, and how it didn't cause an issue. No, Benjamim, he wasn't crazy, he wasn't losing it. Unlike Carmem, I didn't see it that way then, and I still don't. The madness came later, because insanity means that someone can no longer discern reality, and begins instead to create a private reality, one that only he can see. And there in Jequitinhonha, Teo had completely integrated into that society, that place—it's true. He felt that way, and so did they.

Besides that, he hadn't stopped thinking with that slow, intelligent flow he always had. It seemed like while I was getting excited by starting to be able to trace general lines across a broader world, he was going in the opposite direction. To him every detail was a field of infinite research. Every minuscule thing contained everything. It wasn't that feeling of blessed ignorance I experienced, but of certainty about a universe that was growing ever smaller, a specific and profound certainty that makes the heart ache, speechless, like a flash of light. What I'm telling you now is something I could only grasp later, after everything that's happened. His work was more intense and solitary than mine. He wasn't going crazy, only distancing himself from me and from everything I knew. The world that had been ours together was no longer mine, and even less his.

Maybe it's hard for you to understand how frightened I was, because you didn't know Teo before Minas. But think about your grandmother, your aunts and uncles. Today, they're all adults, they're getting old—maybe none of it sounds unusual. But that house took a steep toll. I don't want to be unfair, because Isabel and Xavier raised their children in accordance with their beliefs. Freedom was something to fight for. They thought they could always keep a handle on things—they never guessed that the very worst could happen to one of them. With Flora, the fucking craziest one of all, they had to go looking for her in the middle of the night, tear her from the jaws of strangers. They put up with her freewheeling friends, who stayed for weeks at a time in the house, they accepted her decision to cut school for months so she could travel with a theater troupe that had nothing to do with Xavier's delicate sort of art. By the time you came to live here in São Paulo, that house no longer existed, and neither did your grandfather.

I was no use, it was a confusing time. My first kid was about to be born. I distanced myself and didn't help Teodoro—I couldn't, I didn't want to, I left Isabel there, stuck with the two of you. A widow, a child, and a madman. Haroldo only got in the way and made things worse, but there was nothing I could say. How could I blame him? I was the one who fell away. I can only imagine how difficult it was for her to start going crazy on you, too. She ended up taking care of you all by herself, and I have no idea what your adolescence with her was like.

I know you're not Isabel's son. Times have changed and now we all have other concerns. Don't get short with me, Benjamim, I'm not asking anything of you. It was you who came looking for me. You don't have to apologize. I know you get annoyed by any mention of your grandmother, or if I place you at the center of the narrative. I guess you're fed up with the sort of blathering we were all so proud of back then, and now that the old dreams are dead, all this must seem rather decadent to you. But this nostalgia isn't mine, it's your family's—they lived all of it so intensely. And "all of it" was only the formation of their children, the creation and dissolution of that illusion of a different sort of family, a special family. Okay, I write, I'm a screenwriter, and I might have my vices. It's late, I'm tired, and I've been drinking, but that's not the issue: if you listen, you'll see that I'm really talking about your father. What I'm trying to fucking tell you is if you don't understand the world he was inhabiting, then everything is just going to seem like some stupid shit that happened to some deadbeat who went looking for some kind of rustic wilderness and went nuts the minute he had to confront the primitive side of rural life.

The problem, Benjamim, is that lurking in your question there's a veiled accusation—or several. Of course, you're right to be pissed at finding out now that Isabel knew all along who your mother was. She didn't want your aunt Leonor to show you the other Benjamim's birth certificate, either, when she was putting your grandfather's papers in order. I know you have scores to settle. But what you haven't realized is that my scores aren't settled either—not even with myself. You know what I mean?

Teo was in detox, ridding himself of the vocabulary and the notion that he was special. This was the price he had to pay, not only because of his family, but also because of the schools we went to. Talk, talk, talk, explain, argue, debate. In my house, at least, I still fought with my brothers, and from time to time we resolved things by kicking the shit out of each other. I did things on the sly, and at the table we could just sit quietly while the adults talked. At the Kremz house there was never a break in the action. That's why I thought they were perfect. I never saw anybody hit anyone else, and nothing was done on the sly. In that house you had to learn how to debate, you trained to be precise, and had to be ready with an opinion on every single issue. From age eight to sixty, we were adults, all of us—with all the same expectations, judged to the same standards. Irony was incentivized, good Portuguese was essential. Clichés, imprecision, and obvious statements were punished with a refined and perverse sarcasm. Thinkers and artists came into fashion, their names were elevated, especially by Isabel, but months later they'd be back in limbo. She was always looking for something—an explanation, a new vision ... I don't know what it was. When she found it, she seemed satisfied in a half-obsessive, euphoric way, and she requested that we use our meeting of the minds to untangle and then annihilate the new gospel.

After everything that happened with Teo, I started to recall those days of our adolescence, and saw in them the inception of the virus that unchained his illness. It was an illness of that house. There were so many stimuli, and I only saw a richness of spirit—the only dark spot was me, because I could never rise to their level of understanding. Everything that rhetoric made elegant was true, from Silvio Santos to Erik Satie. Elegance had to do with a precise logic of argumentation, a sophisticated aesthetic. It had to do with class, too, with high culture, pop and provocation, millennia of traditions, refinement, and exclusion.

Teo told me that during the first month of his voyage, he was vomiting constantly and had diarrhea. The spitting habit came later. He became a dirty man, spitting on himself. He didn't bathe and had dusty knots in his hair. I couldn't imagine Teo this way in 1977, in the Jequitinhonha Valley—not until what came later. He said that he decided to cut his hair short, the way people did there, and cast aside his city clothes. He kept only some books, a guitar, and the notebook in which he wrote and drew. He said he felt calm and couldn't stand talking anymore. He wished only to work and play guitar. He didn't even want to think about much, and just let things happen.

All right—fine. But Teo was the most cerebral and cultured in our set. He could be funny, he knew everything, had an amazing memory, and read like nobody else. He wasn't merely intelligent, he was an encyclopedia. He was the type who could tell you how an airplane gets off the ground, the capitals of every country on earth—and all in this annoyingly natural way. He had the mind of a scientist, someone who pursued every detail of the things he wanted to learn. He detested vague affirmations—he wasn't the type of guy to get pulled along. I don't know if Leonor also found your father's notebooks when she cleaned out the house. He transcribed the various folk songs he knew, describing the links and similarities between the different melodies and styles he learned to play. He jotted hypotheses about the geographic features that led to these traditions and transformations in musical form, taking the relative isolation of each village into account, according to its proximity to or distance from the rivers. He drew birds and plants. The notebooks were an outline of his thoughts—they weren't for anyone else to read.

When we were younger, about twelve or thirteen, Teo had a notebook in which he drew comics that satirized our teachers and stuff that happened at school. He and I were also characters, and we always came out victorious. There were women with big boobs who wore anklets and had red fingernails, scenes full of blood and violence. It was funny. There was a really boring science teacher, Dona Vanca, whom he portrayed as an earthworm with shriveled breasts that dragged on the ground. She had heart-shaped purple lips and a black cobra tongue, forked and glistening; she groveled for our affection, curling around our legs and panting like a dog. Your father's character would give her a kick and yell no! never!

31

you're condemned to asexual reproduction until the end of time! I've told you a thousand times, and I won't say it again! Then Dona Vanca split into wormy pieces all over the floor, becoming a whole gang of Dona Vanquinhas, squirming and begging for love. We'd smash the worms and under our sneakers with untied laces, smush them into a bloody goo full of little purple mouths, pleading: more, more, yes, just a little more. There were all kinds of other crude things, way worse than that. Anyway, they were stories—with Teo everything fit into a story. Until it didn't. Maybe I just couldn't find the thread because I was no longer a part of the story. The relationships between various melodies, his drawings of birds and plants, everything that he put in those notebooks: it was just what remained of his old habit, and not something that interested him any longer.

The drawings were beautiful. He'd changed the way he sketched: it was looser, more personal. He wanted to know all about songs and their relationships to each other. He'd start telling me about it but then stop. My interest made him self-conscious. "The wrong words," he'd say, "that's not what's important. The words aren't what makes the song, it can be just breath, a few sounds, enough to maintain the meaning of what takes shape inside me. Thoughts come undone into things with no importance." He'd say that actually, thoughts had no importance, none at all, and this was the problem with talking: the pretense of turning something real into something else, something less substantial than the slightest breeze. Chopping wood, putting up fences, killing pigs: this actually mattered. Because anyone could do those things, anyone honest and willing—and they always got done. But trying to articulate why those things were so important— even that was foolish. That's why he seldom spoke.

So that's how he was with me. With others there he was a real talker, a bit of a joker, something he'd never been before. And it's funny: the certainty that he was special—it was still there and had maybe gotten stronger. Only from then on he wanted to be special with his hands. He wanted people to judge him by what he made and not by what he'd been but could never stop being. It wasn't working. Remembering all this makes me sad—sad about how angry his pride in being simple made me, because his search was something real, and it's sad that he never managed to free himself from the curse of his birth. Here in São Paulo your father would get on my case if I pronounced a word incorrectly in English, if I mistook the name of a song or something like that—whenever I said or wore or did something that demonstrated my desire to be something I wasn't, at least not yet. Do you understand what I mean? Sometimes, in that house, I felt like the ugly duckling, so gauche, helplessly inept. I didn't have the right upbringing, the right breeding. I hadn't suckled that milk. And now, telling you about those feelings has caused them to return with a vengeance. I feel the weight of that curse you bear. I'd like to be clearer. To speak with the wise distance of age. But you, Benjamim—you reembody that. Something to do with your mouth, the way you lower your eyes with that angry laugh, even without meaning to. I'm being totally open with you because I know that's what you came for—it was there, too, between your mother and father. No, please, it's not a criticism: I only want you to see that this luminous isolation still remained with your father in Minas, and there's still a well of resentment here in me, as I speak to you. I want you to know that, so you can filter whatever I tell you through this understanding.

The fact is that Teo began to be ashamed of my company,

my long hair, my way of talking and staring. I could tell I was tarnishing his image in the village. I got fed up. Those months we'd spent apart helped me develop the critical autonomy I needed to understand that Teo's judgments rang false. They only had truth for him, and didn't apply to anyone else. At the same time, I'd missed him like crazy. He was my best friend, and there were moments when we still really connected. Like the time we went to kill a pig at Mr. Nestor's. He was one of Teo's guitarist friends, a widower who lived with his unmarried daughter and a slew of grandkids. Teo lent a hand with some of their livestock chores and anything else that might be hard for a woman and an old man to do by themselves. Usually when someone wanted a pig slaughtered, they got a bunch of people together, because it was so many chores in one: killing the pig meant flaying it, carving it, cleaning it, separating the parts to be salted and preserved. It was customary to offer parts of the pig to anyone who came to help, get them drunk, anyway, an expensive ritual for the old man. Aside from that, there were actually very few men around the village during the day—they'd leave in the morning looking for work somewhere else. The plantations in the region hadn't had a good crop that year, and there was a general fear that things might continue this way. Teo had already gotten used to eating very little and refusing the polite gestures and gifts that the villagers, even as they starved, never stopped offering. It took me a while to understand the subtleties of it all. People thought it was funny: the way that I, a well-fed city boy, was always famished.

I'd never killed a pig and never witnessed the slaughter of an animal. I wanted to help, and tagged along with the idea of simply following Nestor's and Teo's instructions. The pig wasn't really fat enough to slaughter, but there were small children who needed meat so they could grow. Outside, next to the house, near the kitchen, we set out a wooden table for gutting the animal. The children were tasked with holding a bowl to collect the blood. Maria, the daughter, and Mr. Nestor held the pig's legs while I held its head. Teo plunged the knife in. There was a lot of blood, a lot of noise. A wild squealing that I felt all the way down to my stomach—my stomach and my guts. The animal shook its head powerfully, suffered a few violent spasms, and then went limp. My legs gave out. I could barely keep from vomiting as Teo ran the knife from the pig's neck down to its tail. Watching, stunned and stupid, I clenched the pig's head to keep from falling. The strong, hot odor of red entrails gushed out. There was so much life in that death. With the animal dead and still, I sat on a bench and leaned against the kitchen wall, spattered with blood. I stayed there, dazed, my body limp and my eyes open, watching Teo flay the pig. Your father took pleasure in that, in his precise gestures. He slipped his hand inside and pulled out one organ after the next. It must've been hot inside. The oldest child, a shriveled little boy, helped pull out the intestines and bladder—a horrible smell. I remember his little hands and delicate fingers washing the fleshy sacks, then stretching them over the fence to dry. It was a cheerful occasion, an activity in which everyone participated. They knew the correct sequences. You father was happy, concentrating on organizing the party. Slumped down on that bench, I felt their joy: it was good to see Teo like that, a beautiful young man, full of strength.

Isabel

Men, as you know, Benjamim—men like to use their imaginations and tell tall tales. Around the time that Xavier fell in love in Elenir, I didn't know him very well. We hung around a lot of the same places and our families knew each other. That was it. The world was smaller then, and he called attention to himself. Maybe I did too, like Haroldo told you, but I don't think so. Maybe they noticed me because I was a girl from a good family. In those days, only girls who had to work went to college.

These days in the hospital. This green room. It's confusing for things to be brought to a halt like this. It's never happened to me before, not even after I retired. I continued advising students, I kept writing and participating in panels and discussions. I've always kept myself busy, and I'm not the type to get sick. Even after giving birth I was on my feet two days later, running up and down the stairs. Now there are days I barely speak, my memories come from far off, from long before I had children. Be patient, Benjamim, there's something I want to tell you.

I remember that in my day it wasn't so "good"—in the most irritating sense of the word—to be a serious girl, to focus on one's studies. It wasn't good for boys, either. Young women barely ever considered going to college, and many of the boys went as an afterthought. Today when I see the concentration you put into your studies, your struggle to obtain a fellowship to get a master's degree in the United States, all the specialization, the effort put into being a good professional—this is all new. It simply didn't exist in my generation, because we were all the children of people who owned farms or banks or factories. Very few of my classmates went to Sedes, which had a very good program at the time. It was where my mother studied, first in her class, and at that time it was just for girls. Most girls went to Lareira. There was no such thing as specialization, and the girls just fooled around, waiting for a husband. They learned housekeeping and had a few murky sex ed classes—that kind of thing. The most chic families, and there were only a few, sent their girls to finishing school in England or Switzerland. Those girls learned how to be polished.

My great exception was having gone to USP—that was a complete novelty. Daddy, your grandfather, was an ophthalmologist, a professor on the medical faculty. He knew Dr. Emanuel Kremz from there. We weren't a rich family, but we were a "good" family, and that was what mattered. The other day I rewatched *The Great Gatsby* on TV and got to thinking about the difference between the two. The American upper class between the two wars had something savage to it, in many respects. The thirst for amusement, the vanity and ostentation. The girl says something like, "Rich girls don't marry poor boys," as though it were common sense. We'd never have said that here. We didn't talk about money: we saw it, we knew about it, but it wasn't what made the difference. The difference came from somewhere else.

Now, at home Daddy didn't have the slightest doubt I'd go to college. But this was an oddity in our milieu. Even if I hadn't been the only child, I know that he'd have thought the same thing. It wasn't only about educating his daughter, but had something to do with his different vision for the world. He'd say, "I'm not going to leave you any money, but I'm going to provide you with a good education."

I enjoyed my studies. I wanted to major in philosophy, and Daddy said I could do that at Sedes, never at USP, or else I'd lose my faith. But I wanted to study at USP, so I decided to major in classics. It was an excellent choice. I was reading all the time. I adored college: it was a completely new world for me, because I'd been in the same school from seven to seventeen, the age I was when I started at USP. I was also terrified, because Daddy would say, "If you're going to study at USP, you'd better work hard, because you're coming from a private school and will have to compete against people from the state high schools, which are much stronger." So you see there's been an absolute revolution. Now, of course, what he told me wasn't completely true, because I'd had the opportunity to study English and French. I got in on the first try and did very well at college. The truth is that the curriculum the nuns developed at Des Oiseaux had actually been quite good.

College was a crucial transition for me. Everything was stimulating. The new building—my class was one of the first at the Maria Antonia campus—the foreign professors, classmates from other cities, with different customs. The war had just ended two years earlier, the fascists had been banished from the face of the earth, we lived in a free and prosperous world, in need of hands and minds to build and teach. It was a lot different from the college experience my children had, and much more that what you did. I think the important thing—besides the changes to the role of the faculty, the spatial reorganization, and the ghettoization of departments—besides all that, there was, for us, at the end of the 1940s, that experiential gap between high school and college. It was brutal. I came from a Catholic school. I'd never sat in a coed classroom, and the way the teachers addressed the students was totally different. It was like I'd suddenly been set free from a cloister.

When I went back to school in the mid-sixties, I tried to recapture that feeling of liberation. But everything was so chaotic then, and getting worse every day. The pleasure I took in my studies derived less from a collective experience, and became more solitary. In '77 or '78, when Teodoro decided to take that trip, many professors were still exiled. The environment was one of fracture and frustration, sometimes resentment. I knew he wouldn't really be missing much. Maybe that's why I considered Teodoro's path to be more courageous than the ones his siblings took.

My youngest children were still little at the time of the coup, when the dictatorship started. I imagine that the fear that disseminated throughout the country had some kind of psychological effect on them. I know this because I lived through the war as a girl. There was always the danger of German submarines, blackout drills, my father listening to news about troop movements on the radio. Even though we were so far away, we still felt the imminence of violence, and that left some kind of impression on us all. Back then we were convinced that good had achieved an unequivocal triumph over evil. You couldn't say the same about the feelings of fear and dread that your father's generation absorbed. My generation never had any doubt about our role in the world: it had been destroyed and needed us to rebuild it. Your aunts and uncles and father came of age in very different times. Flora fell into all that hippie stuff, which might have been more violent than politics. The dark and omnipotent suicidal side that every adolescent feels emerged in her use of her body, drugs, and sex.

What I feared was that near-perversion of her body. In my mind, I paced back and forth, trying to find the pathways I could use to watch over her, and somehow, protect her. Her path was different from mine, and I never liked drugs. The truth is I was always afraid—I have such an addictive personality. I smoked my whole life, and it's only now, after winding up in this hospital, that I finally quit. I still crave a smoke—but I don't know if it's worth it anymore. If you'd asked me, I'd have said a girl who smokes pot and has sex is already a woman, able to fend for herself. But it turns out that's not true. Somehow she survived. She got to experiment with things she thought were important and then get on with her life.

Henrique, always the most sensible one, decided to join the workers' movement, and then the Workers' Party. Our house was full of red flags. Your grandfather got irritated with all the rah-rah about the metalworkers, and then with the intellectuals who'd joined the Party project, and with the Party's links to the Catholic Church. He'd always distrusted missionaries. He argued with Henrique. Xavier's field was art. He said he didn't want to be oppressed by avalanches of orderly pronouncements. He wanted disorderly words—always. Half-baked and incoherent speech. He reacted with physical aversion whenever he felt trapped. He was very clever about deconstructing the things we said and revealing our lies. Smooth, implacable, and irresponsible. He was compelled to negate things, even if there was never anything to put in their place. That's why Daddy never really got along with Xavier. And it's why I admired him. I was fascinated by his freedom to criticize without any obligation to be constructive, a position that was always inaccessible to me, I was too weighted down by my obligations to do battle. Xavier liked to be around younger people but didn't want to have anything to do with disciples.

Haroldo says that at college everything was the other way around—he was a leader involved in politics at every level. After his crisis and the trip to Europe, he changed completely. When people started to be persecuted and arrested after the coup, he suffered a great deal. We took in friends and strangers; he was disgusted by the brutalities. I was more worried about holding the house together, keeping us in the black. We were so different—perhaps that's why our marriage lasted as long as it did. I don't know, maybe because he trained as a lawyer and worked at a newspaper, he took a more skeptical view of the motives and methods of the opposition movements. He argued with Henrique, telling him he was unlearning how to think for himself.

Flora mutilated her body and Henrique his intelligence. But those are the rites of passage. Something I know nothing about—how could I?—and even if I did, I wouldn't have known how to act differently . It's just that some don't survive. I say I wouldn't have done anything differently because they took the necessary steps to forge their characters as individuals. What right would I have to impede, restrain, or stifle them? At first, it's necessary to behave like spokesmen of ever more exclusive tribes. Only after that can one's own voice emerge, and return to the rest of humanity. To one's family and generation, and then to the great ideas that germinate the voice that will need to run its own course if it's ever going to be considered original. Only the originals matter, only they can light the way, only those truly unparalleled voices can begin to find new peers. I never wanted any of my sons to be butchers. I wouldn't know how to guide them. Because that's part of it: parents learn alongside their children. They can't do everything. No, Benjamim, there's nothing cerebral to it, in the unromantic sense of the word. Quite the opposite: what could be more generous than discovering your own unique strengths and placing them at the service of others? That's what I'm talking about. This is the moral obligation that I tried to pass on to my children and to you, my grandson.

I married young, in 1954. Getúlio Vargas had just killed himself—it was terrifying to see the masses in the streets, crying for their sweet daddy, their father figure. It wrecked my ideals. I'd gone into the streets demanding his resignation. To see people feeling so orphaned was a shock. I thought that maybe I'd been mistaken, that the truth is always where the people are. Then came Juscelino, and my children. I didn't know a thing about education. I only felt that I needed to stay by my children's side at all times. My experiences wouldn't suffice as a model. We had to start from scratch. And the truth is that no matter how diligent and responsible I was, I never knew anything about life. Nobody knows anything about life until they have children. Xavier always had an opinion about what was best for the children. He was an enthusiastic father, but his sort of dedication was never much help. We had four kids in five years. Flora was born in '55, and Teodoro in 1960. We lived in a little house off Dr. Arnaldo Avenue. After your great-grandfather died, Dona Silvia decided to move back to Higienópolis—she never liked living in the sticks, as she called it. So we took the house in Butantã, which was near the university and the kids' school. With the house and the inheritance everything got a little easier. When your father was two years old, I went back to school, and later began to teach. Back in the same building at the Maria Antonia campus. It was a tumultuous period: first the coup and then the resistance movements. Even in that difficult climate, among the new teachers they brought in, I was able to find my peers. I was happy. During those years when I'd stayed home to take care of the kids, my life was something primordial, animalistic. Giving birth, breastfeeding, washing and cleaning, warding off danger. When I went back to school I returned to myself. In a family we're always a me or an I who's scattered and complex. It's only at work, especially work that has to do with ideas, that it's possible to feel ourselves out and let the contours assume a shape. Xavier's occupational vagrancy made me afraid. I miss him: his joy, the fun we had together. But I was afraid.

Xavier frittered away our inheritance on insane luxuries and that business of printing cheap books. We were the one of the first families with a TV. We also had one of those reel-to-reel tape recorders, the kind people used before cassettes. Xavier used it to record the children singing rounds, as well as the stories that Vanda, the nanny, would tell them. I began to realize that besides going back to school, I'd also have to go back to work if I wanted to keep the kids in good schools. While I was doing my master's, I got a job as a teacher at the kids' school, which meant they could all go for free. They were always good students.

Sometime later Flora bought a Super 8 camera. I don't know what she ended up doing with her little films. She'd invent scenarios and get Leonor and your father to act them out. I think they all enjoyed it, but who knows. There was always so much going on in that house. Henrique and Flora talked incessantly. Leonor was calmer. She made up stories about her dolls and stuffed animals, and practiced piano for hours on end. Teodoro was independent; even as a child he never liked sitting on anyone's lap. He was a quiet boy, very attached to Leonor. The two of them would play by themselves all afternoon. During our vacations at the beach, they'd build sandcastles. When Xavier could join us, he'd create make-believe drawbridges, underground lakes, and traps for enemy crabs. I spent my time reading. On vacations I unwound by reading novels—something I didn't have time for when classes were in session. Back then I could still sleep in, what a pleasure. Vanda would leave early with the kids and bring them back with their arms full of seashells. Teodoro was so cute when he was three, four years old. When he was nine he built a special box for his seashell collection, noting the date he found each one and separating them by size and color. Always so meticulous, traipsing around with his Boy Scout manual. It's true: he always had that passion for collecting and cataloging. At our house here in São Paulo he caught animals, played with armadillos, investigated anthills. We pretended that he was going to be the family scientist.

When I brought you both back here and had him committed, I didn't recall any of that. But his hoarding of trash from the streets was similar to what he'd done with the shells. The same goes for that mania for cataloging. I don't know how much you remember of that period in your father's madness. He, who was always so beautiful, became skeletal, his face sunken in. I missed Xavier, but don't know if he could've handled it. It wasn't easy, Benjamim, it wasn't an easy decision to have him locked up. Henrique helped me with everything. And Haroldo, too, against Raul's wishes. I know that he was angry with Haroldo and felt guilty that he couldn't stick things out with Teo. But he shouldn't have felt anger or guilt—at the time, there was nothing else to be done. Trying to help someone who doesn't want to be helped is the most difficult thing in the world. It means forgetting about forgiveness, which is just something made of words, with no muscle or meat to it. Now that you're an adult, about to have your first son, you seem ready to listen. In those days, and afterward, with everything that happened, you lived with me in my apartment like it was just a room in some boardinghouse. Yes, I know. In the end it was good for you to move out, into a real boardinghouse. You always wanted to be from Minas, you never gave that up. I know, Benjamim, I know that you *are* from Minas. You know what I mean.

I'm talking about the responsibility to be who you are. You're from this family, so you *are* this family. Your father wanted to be rid of all that, and shed himself along with it. The history that he crafted for himself in Minas was a non-history. He went too deep. By the time I brought him back, there was nothing left to hold onto, no handle I could use to hoist him back out: only damaged pieces. You survived just fine. You grew up drinking milk fresh from the cow, catching birds—you enjoyed the simple, humble lifestyle that befalls a field hand's son. You were raised by the kindness of those women, in the hidden spaces of that big plantation house, on that dark cot belonging to your father, a servant in the brickyard of that yes-sir world. You rejected the new atmosphere I offered you. You wanted to say "Yes, ma'am" to me and I wouldn't have it. No, Benjamim, you were never rude to me. On the contrary: you had perfect manners. We were locked in a battle between different rubrics of politeness. Nobody won, nobody lost, and there was no truce. That's where we left it.

Now that you're back, handsome as always, soon to be a father, you need to understand something that was always here between us and will also be with your son. I'll probably never meet my great-grandson, little Antonio, but you will doubtless recognize me in him—your father, too. That's why you came—that's why you need to understand. This search has nothing to do with your mother. She was never from here. I have nothing to say about her. But I can tell you about your father, and we can each talk about ourselves. About how you were before you'd reached adolescence: about that clever and lively little boy with shining eyes. About me, and how I dragged a man from the abyss, the man who would never again be my "prodigal son."

During that time your father was still with us, with all the comings and goings from the clinic, and with me still finishing my tenure file, you became a little ghost, tiptoeing throughout the house and hiding in the corners. Maybe you don't believe it, but I worried about you. I worried a lot.

Haroldo

Xavier was still half-loony when they released him from the sanatorium. He was bloated, slow: still impregnated by that atmosphere. I went to visit him a few times while he was committed. The clinic was on a farm near São Paulo. They didn't call it a sanatorium, but a "rest home" or something like that. It reminded me of a country club: tall trees, rooms that opened onto the grounds, gravel pathways that wove between ironwood and flamboyant trees. A lake with teal ducks and neatly trimmed grass. It made everything that much sadder. If the place had the look of a hospital about it, if it were a little less clean, if the air a little stuffier—the contrast with my friend's state of being wouldn't have shocked me so much. They'd shaved his head, I guess for the electroshock therapy. He was swollen, his face a full moon. He looked like a little idiotic child. It pained me to see him like that—he was such a handsome young man, barely twenty years old, and a boy for whom beauty was always so important.

A few times I went with your great-grandparents. That was even harder than going by myself. Dona Silvia imbued herself with the same Christian piety that seized her every Friday, at home with the other ladies, knitting sweaters for the children of single mothers. She used to say how during the revolution of '32, she helped cook for an entire battalion, that she cracked more than two hundred eggs in a single day. Ever since then she bore a grudge against one of the Prado Valente girls, because you had to break each egg in a little bowl and only then add it to the pan, and this dumb girl breaks an egg right into the pan and ended up mixing a bad egg in with more than fifty good ones. So they had to throw them all out, a total waste. And during a time of rationing and thrift, she'd say, still indignant, when women pawned their wedding rings for the good of São Paulo.

She was on the shorter side, but held herself so erect that she seemed tall, thin, and elegant. She'd helped your great-grandfather raise the money to start the hospital and directed a ladies' volunteer society. She was an objective, intelligent, and electric person. Always ready with a word to say to everyone—a kind deed, a caring gesture. Every year until she died, I received a little note of congratulations on my birthday, written in the calligraphy she learned from French nuns. She said she had a notebook in which she wrote the names of people who'd been good to her in hard times. She must have also kept a list of those who hadn't. Anyway, everything in the world around her was right, and if it wasn't, it would soon be fixed.

Dona Silvia remembered the nurses' names, brought them little gifts, praising the cleanliness of the clinic and the maintenance of the garden. She made suggestions about new plants and the correct way to prune the rosebushes, and would enter her son's room smiling, with open arms. She'd pat him on the back, straighten the collar on his pajamas, all with a slightly stern maternal air, without infantilizing him. Dona Silvia treated him just like a sane and competent man. She brought him newspapers and magazines, and updated him on the political situation, his friends' careers, family affairs, improvements made to the hospital, and her husband's uninterrupted and insufficiently recognized sacrifices—the prose of a Sunday lunch among healthy adults. One of them not so healthy, of course, and deserving special attention. But she didn't condescend to his condition, and was quick to correct anyone else who did. Better to treat the thing for what it was: a misfortune that, if treated properly, would sooner or later be cured. She always managed to see improvements in Xavier's pitiful state. I started to think that her method might have some positive effect. Pretending that she couldn't see it as her son's downfall could make him believe that he was mistaken: at the end of the day, if everyone was treating him the same as they always had, it was because in some corner of himself, he was still the same as he ever was. Obliging him to keep himself clean, greet people, shake their hands, make small talk—it could activate certain damaged circuits. Pretending that everything was normal, just maybe, I thought, would help him get back to normal. In the mirror that Dona Silvia held up, Xavier was still the man he was before his crisis, before Elenir, before his dead son. It was a combination of her iron determination to wrench her son from that alienation, and her utter refusal to recognize that flabby, ugly man as her son.

The first time we visited together was a week after he was committed. Dr. Emanuel came, too. Xavier remained silent the entire time, his gaze unfixed. Even with the drugs, he hadn't calmed—his eyes constantly darting around the room, his wounded hands rubbing against each other, irritating the raw cuts. The father barely spoke to his son—he didn't even sit down. Instead he had a word with the director of the clinic, who'd received us at the gate with a show of considerate formality. They went over his medications, his behaviors. There were explanations of a favorable prognosis. It was just a question of time. Afterward the director left us alone with my friend. Dr. Emanuel couldn't bear to be there for long, witnessing the spectacle of his firstborn's inexorable madness. He went out for a walk across the grounds, to take advantage of an afternoon in the park. Later it was only I who accompanied Dona Silvia on her visits. Her husband considered his son to be in good hands, and that these family encounters wouldn't help him recover. For Dona Silvia, life revolved around illness, or around health—it's the same thing, really—so she didn't think it was right to neglect her son. But after visiting Xavier a few more times, she was obliged to reach the same conclusion as her husband.

Visits usually took place on the veranda at the sanatorium. Patients and their relatives went for walks in the park, sat on benches beneath trees, or had a soft drink at the tables on the terrace. Xavier refused to leave his room. I remember quite well a certain visit I made with your great-grandmother, probably before the third week—it the last visit she made before heeding her husband's recommendation. The director came with us to his room. As we walked he explained, somewhat haltingly, that the patient was more agitated than usual, still unable to follow a conversation, but able to respond to external stimuli. He said that we shouldn't be alarmed, that when a patient resumed contact with reality, it didn't always go smoothly.

"Xavier suffered a profound trauma," the director said, "He's starting to come back to the surface, but with memories of what dragged him down. This could be a very painful time—one that calls for caution. Don't mention anything that might remind him of the recent past, and above all, don't be alarmed by his words or conduct. He still doesn't have control of himself. This is part of the healing process. We have to be patient and calm."

He opened the door to the room, greeted Xavier, and announced his visitors with a firm tone of voice meant to convey a warning that he behave accordingly. Then he excused himself. I was coming along behind, carrying bags that Dona Silvia had packed full of magazines, clothes, blankets, sweets, notes from Xavier's aunts and cousins. I saw my friend's expression from over the director's shoulder. Xavier was seated on his unmade bed, leaning against the wall with a book in his lap, staring straight ahead at nothing. At the sound of the door opening and of the director's voice, he began to move slowly. There was anger in his eyes. His body stiffened, and he turned to look at the wall. He was completely disheveled: unshaven, barefoot, and wearing his sanatorium pajamas. A prickling of hair had started to grow back on his head. He was still bloated, but looked a little less vacant to me. His concentration, meanwhile, was not directed to his exterior, but toward some dark thought that demanded his strength. If during the first days he was flattened into a shapeless amoeba, two weeks later he had transformed into a compact cocoon.

Dona Silvia gave him a kiss and set about showing him all the things she'd brought. Xavier didn't move his eyes. His mother started finding places for his things around the room, straightening the curtains and puttering. Xavier wouldn't look at the sweets, the blanket, the jacket. He wasn't listening to her telling him about your great-aunt's illness, the birth of his cousin's son, his friend's wedding. He didn't react to updates on state, national, or international politics. Dona Silvia grew quiet, sat down beside him on the bed, and placed a hand on her son's leg. He recoiled and moved away.

Was he reading the Bible? (Silence.) God writes straight through crooked lines. (Silence.) A good son always returns home. (Silence.) Actually, you never abandoned your home.

But lately you've been a bit forgetful. (Silence.) It's probably nothing. (Silence.) Water under the bridge. (Silence.) I recommend the Psalms. In our moments of affliction, direct conversation with God is always soothing. (Silence.) Sometimes, even without our understanding it, just repeating the words, the sound of them is calming, illuminating, bringing consolation. (Silence.) I also recommend Saint Paul's letters to the apostles. But maybe not right now, he's a bit too severe. Is that the complete text? A good translation? Is it a Church bible or one from the Protestants? Let me see who published it. (Xavier moves the book beyond his mother's reach, still staring at the wall. His fingers stroke the delicate pages as though he were marking a rhythm.) Actually I prefer to read the French version, I trust it more. The text might seem simple, but changing just one little word can lose the correct meaning. And the sound of French is so beautiful. (Silence.) I ended up getting used to the Bible in Portuguese because sometimes at the hospital we read it to the patients. Maricota Moraes—she reads very well, and has the patience to explain the passages. Xavier, do you remember your catechism classes? You loved the bolinhos she used to make. Well, she's still at it, calmly negotiating the same ruckus from the children and the ignorance of the poor. Nothing shakes her, she just explains everything in the same slow way. That way the patients can take advantage of the interval of rest imposed by their illness and learn something. They leave more educated. It's beautiful work, what Maricota does. Poor thing, she never married. She had to take care of her sick father and in the end she inherited practically nothing. The prolonged illness ate up whatever was left from when they sold their land. She managed to keep some of the furniture, and she never lost her cheer. In school she was always the liveliest girl. We found out about the latest fashions from Paris by keeping track of the dresses that she and her sisters wore to dances. But that's how it is, we have to be prepared for anything, the world is always changing, and all that's sure to last is the character and education of our upbringing. Thanks to the foresight of Onório Cunha—that's her brother-in-law, Maria Helena's husband—Maricota ended up with some houses that she could rent out to support herself and still play hostess to her girlfriends. That's why we asked her to be the catechism teacher. It was a way we figured we could help without hurting her pride. I remember you and your cousins coming home and laughing about the way she always pronounced every syllable: "Es-ther, a wo-man of un-par-al-leled beau-ty." You liked the more risqué parts of the Bible, and of course the bolinhos. The sick always prefer the Psalms. Especially at sunset, when their fears arise. When you were a baby, you cried a lot around that time of day. I never knew what to do. You'd start wailing and God only knows what was wrong. It never helped to change your diaper or feed you or anything else. All you wanted was to be on your nanny Doinha's lap. She used to say that some babies were just like that, they cry at the end of the day. She'd pick you up and hold you, then walk back and forth singing a lullaby, and you'd calm down. Do you remember Doinha? (Silence.) Of course not, you were so little when she left. Your father didn't like her; he thought she was spoiling you. Your grandmother didn't like her, either. I think it had something to do with their German background. You know, Haroldo— Dona Silvia decided to continue her monologue by switching interlocutors—my mother-in-law never really accepted the idea of having hired help at home. Emanuel was her only child and she always took care of everything herself. She never understood the Brazilian system. She'd say: more people, more work, more filth. Idle hands do the devil's work. Things like that. God help her, she wasn't a bad person, not at all. I learned a lot from her. She complained that I spent too much—she watched over the house like hawk. She didn't know how we could possibly need so much food, saying it was a waste. At her house everything was always rationed. Wealthy as they were, there was no such thing as luxury. Thrift was almost her religion. Thank God Emanuel isn't like that—he likes being comfortable and well served, everything tasteful. But when it came to our children's education, he followed in his parents' footsteps. Which was good, in the end. Look at Xavier, first in his class at São Francisco the whole time he was there, and now he's twenty-two and already working in the best firm in São Paulo. He was always brilliant, it's true, but without discipline, intelligence doesn't get you anywhere. Hard work comes first, that's how they were raised, and that's thanks to Emanuel and the example he set. And later, later, my dear— turning once more to Xavier—you'll be back at the firm and then who knows what's next? You have your whole life ahead of you—you're just starting out. This isn't a stumble that will wreck your career. (Silence. A Bible page turns.) When you were little and your sister started to cry, you'd say, "There's no use cwying over spiwelled milk." Remember? She wanted to come with me to visit you. She really wants to see you, now that it's all over. Your brother, too. But you father didn't think it was a good idea. We know that everything's fine, that you'd receive them with open arms. I told them that you're being careful after this little slip. I have no doubt that we'll be all together again, as a family. Your dad asked them to wait a little longer. To wait until you were stronger. He thinks that right now it's not good for you to have too many visitors. You need your rest. But it's important for you to know that your brothers and sisters love you. Are you listening, Xavier? Everyone's pulling for you—we're all eager for you to get better. (Bible pages turn.) After all, you're the eldest. You're an example to them. Everyone has a role in the family, and making excuses for ourselves never helps, you know. It's true, being sick is different—there's always things we don't expect, I'm just trying to say that we miss having you at home. We all miss you. What happens to you happens to us, too. Your sister was really shaken up. Just imagine, at school with her classmates, the gossip—anyway, it's a difficult time, and we have to overcome it together, like we always did. You might not be back at home yet, but we have you back, and that's what's important. (Another page, and another, then another, a pause.) What's that passage you're reading that you don't want your mother to hear? You still haven't told me.

Xavier placed his hand over the open Bible in his lap and turned to face his mother. He looked tired. Genesis, he replied, staring at his mother as though he saw something beyond her black eyes. Ah, Dona Silvia sighed with a sort of disappointment, turning away, breaking his gaze, the Old Testament. I don't find it very edifying. Yes, there's Esther, a woman of unparalleled beauty, she said, separating all her syllables before letting out a sad laugh. You were so handsome at your first communion. What chapter are you reading? Xavier muttered back at her, barely containing his irritation.

"Lot left Sodom with his daughters. God transformed his wife into a pillar of salt."

"Ah, yes, because she looked back."

"Because she felt compassion at the screams of pain from those who remained behind. The city burst into flame and burned."

"Against God's wishes. He warned her."

Xavier flew into a rant, fixating his gaze on his mother's

eyes, stuttering at times. He was trying to go faster than his strength allowed:

"Genesis, chapter 19," Xavier continued, "The angel of the Lord issued no warnings. God doesn't warn, he punishes as he likes. They taught it to us wrong. Lot takes his daughters to the next city, one in the same valley. He refuses to flee to the mountain, and asks the angel of the Lord to grant him a favor: to allow him to go a nearby city, which Lot says, 'is a little one.' He says to the angel, 'Oh, let me escape thither, (is it not a little one?) and my soul shall live.' The angel allowed it, and the city was called Zoar, which means it was a little one, nothing. You know why, mother? Why it was so important for Lot to flee into nothing?"

Dona Silvia didn't respond. She stared out the window in silence. Xavier's voice gained a strange fluency and power.

"Because, mother, it's only in nothingness that we're protected from divine wrath. Maricota never told us that. In her books the angels were always tall, blond, and clean. The angels of the Lord, mother, were always dirty travelers, strangers, beggars. Abraham was tempted to negotiate with God, to obtain the salvation of Sodom. Do you know that passage? It's very funny, seriously, it's worth hearing"—he burst out laughing—"you'll see."

Xavier got up and started acting out the biblical dialog. He did Abraham with a foreign accent, the caricature of a merchant Jew, somewhat humpbacked, rubbing his hands and bulging his eyes, staring upwards to where God would be. His God was fat, strong, and had a voice like Santa Claus.

"Because the cry of Sodom and Gomorrah is great, and because their sin is very grievous; I will go down now, and see whether they have done altogether according to the cry of it, which is come unto me; and if not, I will know."

This was God, to which Abraham humbly replied:

"Wilt thou also destroy the righteous with the wicked? Peradventure there be fifty righteous within the city: wilt thou also destroy and not spare the place for the fifty righteous that are therein? That be far from thee to do after this manner, to slay the righteous with the wicked: and that the righteous should be as the wicked, that be far from thee: Shall not the Judge of all the earth do right?"

You see, mother—Xavier continued, pacing from one side of the small room to the other—he addresses God like a business partner when he negotiates with Him. That was how Abraham, so meek and abject, made his play. His interest was saving his cousin Lot. Because with Lot, Abraham had fled his father's house and had gone to Egypt. He went with Sarah, his wife, who at that time still wasn't called by that name, which was given to her later by God. She was called Sarai. In Egypt, Abraham feared that Sarai's beauty would attract attention from men and lead to his disgrace. So he tells Sarai to say she is his sister, and gives her to Pharaoh in exchange for lands, sheep, and prestige. God punishes Pharaoh for living in sin with a married woman by sending the plagues. After discovering the trick that Abraham, then still called Abram, played on him, Pharaoh expels them from Egypt, allowing Abraham to depart with his possessions, fearing the awesome power of that foreign God who punishes the deceived and rewards the man who pimps his own wife. Abram leaves with Sarai, Lot, and all their men and animals. They arrive to the region between Negev and Betel and settle there. But there isn't enough land, and the shepherds begin to fight. Abram summons Lot and tells him, "If thou wilt take the left hand, then I will go to the right; or if thou depart to the right hand, then I will go to the left." Lot went East, always the wrong choice. Lot and his men and his belongings end up on the plain of Jordan, settling in Sodom. And now Abraham, by now renamed by God, tries to save him. And from there the negotiation. God responds, "If I find in Sodom fifty righteous within the city, then I will spare all the place for their sakes."

Xavier hunched his back, rubbed his hands together, and gave a nervous chuckle. He craned his neck and directed his words on high: "Behold now, I have taken upon me to speak unto the Lord, which am but dust and ashes: Peradventure there shall lack five of the fifty righteous: wilt thou destroy all the city for lack of five?"

Tall, fat, and powerful: "If I find there forty and five, I will not destroy it."

"Peradventure there shall be forty found there."

"I will not do it for forty's sake."

"Oh let not the Lord be angry, and I will speak: Peradventure there shall thirty be found there."

"I will not do it, if I find thirty."

"Peradventure there shall be twenty."

"I will not destroy it for twenty's sake."

Knowing his people well, Abraham insists once more: "Oh let not the Lord be angry, and I will speak yet this once: Peradventure ten shall be found there."

"I will not destroy it for ten's sake."

Xavier resumed his own shape, taking long paces as he continued in a grave tone: "And Sodom was destroyed. You know what the Sodomites wanted to do with the Lord's messengers, the ones who were sent to find those ten righteous men? The angels arrived in the guise of foreign travelers, and were met by Lot and taken into his house. The Sodomites surrounded the house and tried to take them out by force so that they could abuse them. They said to Lot: 'bring them out unto us, that we may know them.' It's right there in the Bible, mother. You know what Lot proposed? To give them, instead of the strangers, his two virgin daughters, so that the Sodomites could have their way with them instead. There's a note in this edition that explains: in those days, the honor of a woman was owed less consideration than the sacred duties of hospitality. Afraid of gossip, huh? We're still right by the Bible, then, thank God—what's proper still comes before what's moral."

"Very funny, Xavier, but that's enough." Dona Silvia let out a firm huff, straightened her back, and began folding her bags and collecting her things as a way of marking the end of her visit.

"No, mother, we're just getting started, starting at the beginning, which is the right way to do it. It's necessary to understand this history. Violence, sex, negotiation: it's all there, right at the beginning of everything. A woman's honor and the man's position in society, each on separate sides of the scale. Which is worth more? You always knew, all of you always knew, mother, you read it in the Good Book. Nobody told me. Everything was camouflaged and I believed in the good news of Christ. But the Father is stronger, older, and perseveres at the heart of our cities. All of them."

"Son, you shouldn't make light of these things. It's just not done."

"What's not done? Reading the Bible?"

"Reading it that way. It's not doing you any good."

"But it's the only book they have in this hospital. And good thing it is, amen! Because it's the first book—look, mother, everything starts here. Right down to our laws. Yes, we should have classes on divine law. It's all here, along with justice, the demand for witnesses, sentences, the details of every punishment. If a murder is committed and you don't catch the killer before sunrise the next day, you can't kill him, you have to take him to be judged. If an animal twists its foot in a hole that someone else dug and breaks its leg, what do you do? God tells you the right way to proceed, God gets into the details—everything about humanity interests him. It's here."

Xavier rustled the pages, pointing with his finger, citing chapters and verses, pacing while he searched for the right passage. He laughed and got angry, his mood alternating from one moment to the next. He took his mother's arm, pulled her toward him to read the scriptures, word for word. Dona Silvia was uncomfortable with her son's touch. She delicately removed his masculine hand from her thin arm. She didn't lose control, but she was afraid.

"You know what happened with Lot and his daughters?" Xavier took a deep breath and looked at me with malice. "You know what they did with their old man? Do you know, mother?"

Dona Silvia, resigned and ironic: "No, son, but I'm sure you'll tell us."

Xavier gave a sheepish laugh and stood before us like a child about to recite a poem for adults.

"They were the only ones left, the only chosen ones in the new city they'd fled to. They needed to continue their people's line, and never considered mixing their chosen blood with the blood of the common people. So just look, Dona Silvia, just look at the solution that Lot's daughters found."

Standing in front of his mother, who was still seated on the bed, Xavier pulled down pajama pants and started to masturbate.

"They got drunk and shamelessly fucked their own father. One after the other."

Dona Silvia got up, furious, face to face with her son, locking eyes with him as she hissed, "Enough, Xavier. You've crossed every line. Pull yourself together, boy. Enough of this nonsense. Get dressed right now. You'll never get better if you hide behind this madness. No, sir. Decency and restraint—that's what that girl took from you. I will not tolerate this disrespect, do you hear me? Everything has its limit."

She spoke without raising her voice. Her eyes, her neck, and her mouth fiercely screamed, but the volume of her voice was lower than usual.

"Haroldo, would you be so kind as to help your friend get dressed," Dona Silvia ordered me, picking up her purse and moving toward the door.

I approached Xavier so that I could, at least, pull up his pants. He pushed me away and ran after his mother, laughing and screaming, it's in the Bible, mother, it's in the Bible, I didn't make it up! He tripped over his pants, still around his ankles, and fell flat on the ground. Dona Silvia kept going, without looking back.

Raul

Sorry it's so late. You caught me at a busy time, everyone needs a piece of me. It's been a while since I've had this much work, I can't pass it up. I used to do a line to get through it all. But it got to be too much, cocaine's a bitch. I gave it up. To this day I still have olfactory hallucinations, because it was so good and sometimes life is so hard, so fucking hard. But with a kid and a schedule to keep—time to get up, brush your teeth, tell a bedtime story—I couldn't do it anymore. The comedown got worse and worse, and just made me more and more irritated. Now I stay away from it. Cold turkey, just a few pills to help me along—and wine and vodka. I know you're not planning to stick around for very long, so I don't want to save anything for later. I'm enjoying our conversations. I was nervous when you first called, but shit, it's a huge fucking relief to be telling you all this.

Teodoro was turning into this heavy thing haunting me, and now, talking to you about him, I'm actually enjoying myself. It's not amusing. On the contrary, it's very complicated. I was thinking about this in the car on the way home to meet you. I was thinking that your seriousness, your need to know all about Teo—it's making me see things in a new light. Something to do with the truth. It seems like it's only now that I can bury my friend, let him go back to being something good.

Or bad—I don't know. A spade of lime, a spade of earth, a wreath of flowers.

Out there in Jequitinhonha, before the boat trip up the São Francisco—I told you what he was like there, about our reconnection that didn't exactly connect. The pig, the place. It was nearing the day when we were supposed to go to Pirapora to meet some friends who were coming from São Paulo to ride up the river on a steamer with us. Your father was threatening to stay behind, saying he had work to do: a fence to mend, an addition to build on somebody's house. By this point we'd managed to reestablish a balance between us. The energy of our friendship returned—sort of different, but it was back. One night we went to the home of his Paraguayan lady, which was in the red-light district of a nearby town that was barely bigger than our little village. Actually the red-light district was pretty much just the Paraguayan lady's house. I'd never fucked a whore. I didn't have anything against whores—it just hadn't happened yet. I don't think he'd ever done it back in São Paulo, either. We'd both had girlfriends and girls for friends and everything just sort of worked out. This business with money was vaguely threatening. It messed with my head. Your father was always courteous. He wasn't the kind to brag or fall in love. He'd still never had a steady girlfriend, someone who could get him to loosen up. I think he fucked a lot of girls, and some of them were insulted because they thought it was something more serious. And he, in his intellectual and erudite way, would figure out a way to move on without entangling himself. We didn't talk about sex—we discussed our fantasies, ways to fuck, women we wanted, but never about real experiences. When things started happening for real, we stopped talking about sex or love. It was an explicit agreement. An insistence of Teo's, one that interrupted our conversations about desire. Words ruin anything that's about to happen, he told me in a low voice one hot night, on the upper veranda outside our bedrooms—they turn it into something mediocre. And I agreed. And so for that reason the subject was restricted to the vulgar level of techniques and possibilities, and neither of us found out what the other was up to.

Even though I'd never seen Teo in action, what I saw at the Paraguayan's house was nothing new. Teo let himself love. That's what it was. It was a run-down house, like all the others on that street. The town had a store and a church, and this unpaved street was on the way out of town, before the road and the forest. Mud shacks, some of them unpainted, or crumbling so badly that they blended into the street. Chairs on the sidewalk, mothers combing their daughters' hair, children running, mangy dogs lying around, abandoned lots, a twisted cashew tree, a hen scraping the ground, trash, and women in the windows and out in the street. Men at the bar, a horse tied to a tall stump, an old car with the radio on. We drank pinga and watched a game of pool. On the sidewalk, next to a plastic table where some old guys were playing dominoes, we drank another pinga. Everybody knew Teo. He was wearing serge pants and a white, short-sleeved button-down, his hair combed wet, like a guy out of a film from the fifties. Just like the rest of them. And handsome, your father really knew how to be handsome. And the more he tried to fit in, the more he stood out. Maybe it was just because I'd missed him, and it felt like we were inseparable again. There, in that bar, starting to feel drunk, and with those women's stares making me nervous, I saw your father as though from far away, and I got a bad feeling about things. He was pushing himself beyond his limits, he wouldn't last. Anybody in from the street, I thought, would see that he—even in that getup, and with his darkened skin and that Mineiro accent, which sounded just like everyone else's—they'd see that he stood out even more than me, a white boy from São Paulo with long hair and a pink smock, something nobody there would ever wear. He'd never be just another guy in from the street.

Fine, nobody ever is. I miss him in a way that hurts, and what happened next changed the way I remember this trip. And the guilt I feel. In those days I think I still could've convinced him to come back. But I didn't try. I didn't take my premonition seriously. I wasn't able to interpret it. At first I thought life out there was great. I admired Teo's way of taking an interest in the people and their customs. When I realized it wasn't just a vacation for him, but a search for meaning—it bothered me. I thought that he was putting on an act, that this act was a way of reproaching me. I didn't believe that his new friends—the ones at that bar, for example, or even Mr. Nestor and his family—could really be his friends. What I mean is, they were decent people and everything, but something was off.

At the whorehouse there was an older lady, a younger woman, and a pretty girl. There were other people outside, leading against the wall, talking, swaggering around. Teodoro greeted them with a look, pointed to the one he wanted and went right in, the woman following along behind him. Completely shameless. I just stood there, no idea what to do. The girl stepped forward and offered to take me inside. It was dark and reeked of rotting food. We went upstairs to the girl's room, and she—well, she was more experienced than I was. She had youthful exuberance combined with the gestures of a powerful woman. In the shadows of her room, her gentle, smooth face appeared more like a diabolical mask. She did things nobody had ever done to me before—nice things, really nice. I was afraid of the immense pleasure I felt, of never wanting it to end, of losing control of that pleasure. I felt like dying and killing. Teo came out laughing loudly and I emerged buzzing and empty.

We walked back under a moonless sky rippled with stars. I asked why he preferred the older woman and not the girl. He said that with the girl it was something else. I said she wasn't exactly a child and started telling him about the things she knew how to do. But he got annoyed and said he didn't want to hear it, he already knew all about that. "She's a little sister to me, not a whore. Not to me. You can fuck her and enjoy it—whatever, I don't care, but I don't want to hear about it. I sleep with my other sister and what we do is nobody's business." He kept walking. He was happy. I thought that this was his way of finishing off the tour of his new world, including the parts that would remain secret to me, and that now I could go.

Even so—and I don't know if it was my insistence, or if he still had something to tell me—Teo came with me to Pirapora and then on the trip up the São Francisco. Carmem came, too. By then she was already my girlfriend and he still hadn't met her. She came with Rafael, Helinho, and three other friends, all girls. We went to get them at the bus station and stayed the night in Pirapora at an inn. Teo was his old self again. We drank a lot, and he regaled us with stories about his adventures in a debauched sort of way—there none of that backcountry Minas quaintness from the preceding days. He seemed almost relieved, laughing at dumb jokes, totally at ease and free with his words and his sarcasm. But something was missing, either in him or in the group. But almost a year had passed, and the chemistry of the group wasn't the same anymore. There wasn't the same intelligence, the provocative way of seeing things that conferred a kind of ascendancy over us. It didn't seem to interest us anymore. Unless it was somehow affected by the addition of Carmem—something I started to fear.

On the boat he became even more demonstrative, in an almost aggressive way. I don't know if that old steamboat still exists. It had a wood-burning engine, and from time to time we'd pull alongside the bank so they could cut more firewood. It was a precarious contraption for practical travel between towns up and down the river, hardly a tourist vessel. On the second level there were cabins with cots, and meals served on tables. We were traveling below in second class. We ate right where we slept, on the floor. Having no experience with this kind of travel, we'd brought sleeping bags, which were way too hot, and immediately got filthy. The locals brought hammocks and tied them to the cabin rafters. Teo hadn't brought anything—he'd borrowed some hay and a sheet from the lady who owned the inn at Pirapora. Down there below deck, late on the first day, they hung a sheep by its back legs, killed it, and quartered it for out meals. The blood spattered the floor, attracting flies. It was all part of the fun, we weren't worried about the mess. We weren't worried about anything. In spite of our differences, we got along great with the locals. There was a mutual curiosity, and it obviously helped that we had so many girls with us. We went around all day in shorts, the girls in bikinis. They got deep suntans, and in the towns where we stopped they wore flowered cotton dresses and braided leather sandals.

Teo was our local guide. He found the coolest and most secluded places for us to stay. He knew the customs, the gestures, the argot. He played the guitar, made friends with people who were traveling from port to port. He was at ease, not shy and excited like the rest of us. One by one, the girls ended up with him. Fine. Neca, Filó, and Teresa weren't anybody's girlfriend, and they didn't want to be. It was summer break, they were having fun. They knew Teo. Except for Carmem, they were all his classmates in high school. They knew he was the kind of guy who didn't get too attached, so if they slept with him, that's all they were after. But the fact that he was different, that now he was something of a local or whatever—it excited them. Him, too. He was much more vulgar and macho. He told me about his liaisons, how they each performed, their notable attributes. He showed them off like some kind of shitty playboy would do with a TV actress. With the girls he was ironic, waxing poetic on the primordial animality that inhabited every man and woman, and the pleasure unleashed by the male's power and the female's submission.

Neca ended up getting pissed off and distanced herself from it. Filó and Teresa thought it was all a fun show. They played at competing for Teo's favors like they were women in a harem, seeing who be the most attentive to their lover. Whenever we stopped in a new town, the three of them went out together to visit the market, see the church, have an ice cream, enjoy themselves. The girls were in love with this triangle, every day they were more dependent on Teo, acting like stupid, childish girls. Teresa was training to be an architect and Filó was studying anthropology. Both of them were from more conservative families. Good students, teacher's pets. So when they finally go to let loose, they really went all out.

Things got a little heavy between us. Their little show required an audience, and the rest of us weren't in the mood to play along. Sometimes all eight of us would be together, sitting on the floor playing cards during the day, or listening to Teo play the guitar in the evening, which was quite nice. Whenever he picked up the guitar, he was back to being a good guy. It was like that until the end. Even at the very end—after he came back to São Paulo and brought you along, when I thought that there was no possible way for us to communicate anymore, the two of us living in separate universes without any possibility for contact—even then, many years later, whenever he picked up the guitar, something different happened. His body would relax, he seemed to empty himself and flow through his fingertips, down into the strings and the wood of that guitar. It was something generous, communal. After moments like that on the boat, he'd wander off by himself. Sometimes he'd be chatting with the crew, listening to their stories. He didn't want his women around.

With Carmem he was still the serious boy from São Paulo. They talked about philosophy and literature. He told her about life in Minas in a lower tone, one I knew was more sincere. It made me nervous. I admired the Teo he sharing with Carmem so much that I had no doubt she'd fall in love with him. It seemed impossible that she wouldn't. My only advantage was that I got there first, I thought, and one of the boundaries that I was beginning to doubt Teo still respected. I don't know, Benjamim, but to give you an idea of how important and confused my relationship to your father was, I started thinking that if Carmem didn't fall in love with him on that boat trip, I'd be disappointed in her somehow. I was certain that she was the love of my life—and in fact she was. And like an idiot I'd already told her how amazing Teo was, before the trip. We'd only been dating for a little while, but I already knew that things with her were more serious than they ever were with other girlfriends. I was careful with how delicate she was. She had some things in common with Teo: they both took everything so seriously, and delighted in details other people never noticed. But she wasn't so tightly wound. She didn't have anything to prove to anyone. Maybe that's natural for a pretty woman, which she always was, that cheerful calm before the world—carefree. So disarmed and intelligent, she sometimes took offense to silly things. I was scared to death of losing her, and it was happening right before my very eyes. I didn't want to lose my cool—I let them talk and went swimming by myself. One day I made a stupid joke about the harem of Pasha Teodoro, including Carmem by implication. That son of a bitch just chuckled to himself and Carmem was so offended I thought she'd never speak to me again, the biggest idiot in the world. She went the whole day without talking.

I'm telling you this crazy story because it came just before the tragedy that happened on that trip, which led to your father's reclusion. Actually I didn't even mean to tell you. I thought I could tell you everything else and skip over this part. Now you know. I wasn't with him when it happened. We only ever got Teresa and Filó's side of the story. Okay, so all throughout the trip the three of them seemed like they were role-playing, like a stud and two of his bitches. They thought it was funny, as I told you, to display themselves like that, the whole thing was an amusing piece of theater to them and whatever. But one day, after Filó turned up with a black eye, smiling like some lowlife's girlfriend, the rest of us realized that things were getting out of hand. Neca was furious and had a talk with her, but Filó said it was what she wanted, that she made him do it—she said she wanted go all the way to the extreme, that we had no idea how hot it was, and that we should stay out of it. There was no way of talking to Teo.

He laughed and said it was nothing like that. Filó must have slipped and hit her face on a sharp corner or something. He said that women who liked being hit were vulgar. "I detest that kind of vulgarity," he'd said, laughing in Filó's direction. She was staring at him, lovelorn.

Carmem didn't cultivate any of that pseudomysticism about being open to the world and whatever may come. She thought it was all a bunch of idiotic rhetoric. She distrusted any worldview that excluded other people a priori—"Anyone who's never slept in a sleeping bag hasn't truly ever experienced what it means to sleep"—that sort of thing. Maybe that's why she was the first to intuit the madness in this game Teo was playing with Filó and Teresa, and was the first to show concern. Teo spoke with her about it. Carmem told me that he needed help, that we had to do something. I was blinded by jealousy. I knew that she liked taking care of people, and I interpreted her concern as another risk to our relationship. I didn't want to take her view into account. I said it was all a charade, they were just having fun, trying new things, experimenting with rough sex—sex and violence are always intertwined—and that anyway, who cares if somebody wants to be a slut? As I was talking, I remembered that half-demonic girl I had sex with, the pleasure I took in her violence, the way she seemed a thousand times more in control of her body than I was of mine. At the same time, I also remembered the tone of Teo's voice when he told me, "For me she's not a whore." I realized that he completely despised whores. For him, there was nothing liberating about it—and not for the woman either, because it was a form a humiliation. I tried to imagine how Filó and Teresa must have looked through his eyes and it was just awful. He was humiliating all of us with that little act. Carmem spoke about it with a mix of pity and worry.

The next night we anchored. There was a problem with the boat's engine and the replacement part would only arrive in the morning the following day. So we were stuck in Bom Jesus da Lapa, a depressing little town in Bahia with not a lot going on. The town was a site of pilgrimage and devotion, with a claustrophobic cave where a bunch of people displayed their wounds in a dark, smoky grotto full of ex-votos: legs, arms, and organs made of wood, portraits, little notes. I wanted to go back to the boat. The smell of fermented flesh seemed like it was penetrating my skin. Carmem came back with me while the others explored the town.

After my stupid joke about Carmem being part of Teo's harem, the two of them started keeping their distance, and the last trace of the old Teo we had known in São Paulo finally disappeared. Carmem said I'd given him a signal to start seeing her as another easy woman. Being treated that way in front of a guy who was already on the edge of the abyss—it put her in the same category as the other girls: proud sluts. Then she told me about the crazy things Teo was saying about the other girls he called "the Paulistas." It went more or less like this: "Why don't they wear bikinis to ride the bus in São Paulo? How come they don't sunbathe at building construction sites? Why do they have such contempt for the men here? What gives them this assurance? Do working-class men come through these parts carrying flour to the market and coming back with salt, coffee, and two yards of cloth for their wives, just so they can trip over a fully grown woman lying around on the ground having some kind of communion with nature? That man is part of nature's temptation—but excluded from their cosmic integration. He burns quietly, burns with rage, and he will have his revenge. And there she is, wearing a thin veil over her browned skin while she wanders around intrigued by the fertility of the markets, reeking of jackfruit and piss. She goes to see nativity scenes in old colonial houses, smiling as she accepts a glass of jenipapo moonshine from the lady of the house, and says she likes the simplicity of the little town chapel, squats in the doorway of a bar to down a beer and laugh because all communication is possible, because as a Brazilian woman she's part of those beautiful and ancient pieces of lives, her heart quickening when she cackles at the men's jokes. We're all one family, she thinks, and life is simple." And Teo—Carmem told me that night on the silent, motionless boat—thinks that this joy is offensive. Their lack of fear was a lack of respect. "Who are these women? Just beauty and power, a nice smelling thing drifting by. They're skin, tits, pussy—their white-girl way of walking and laughing. It's the body that communicates—it's at the core of everything, these transactions—they're our bodies, on both sides. A tree branch, a butterfly in flight, a stone in the street, wet lime, a hand rolled cigarette. That's what the people here are to city girls, and that's what they are to the people here: a galloping horse, pretty colts to look at—and ride, if the occasion arises. That's why they're just tramps, weightless beings—but charming, in the way the chapel, the jenipapo liquor, and the smell of jackfruit are to them. Just the escapades of girls on vacation. But the people don't leave, and the chapel stays where it is, and the houses have owners, there's no break or vacation and nothing is simple. That's why they need to feel things with their bodies, they need to be wounded and dominated: it makes them unique, experiencing something that belongs to them and no one else—even if that something is pain and blood, it gives them a face and a name, a soul."

Filó said that the three of them were at a bar and one of

the villagers, an older guy, came over to join them. He started talking to Teo, telling him things about the pilgrims, that he had a truck he used to take people to the cave on holy days. He rambled about the miracles the faithful repeated as lore. The four of them were all drinking beer. At first the guy would only look at Teo, talking just to him. Then the girls joined the conversation and he realized it was okay for him to look at them and talk to them, too. Then came a discussion of who everyone was, questions about how a man could have two women, if one of them was really single, and Filó told him that everything was cool, they were just having fun. Teo said that he didn't own anyone, they were just two sisters enjoying themselves. And the guy wanted to know if maybe there might be some left over for another one of God's children. They all laughed and then got quiet. Teo looked at the girls, Filó said, and asked them: all right, sisters, what do we do for a man in need? Filó said that right then she sobered up with fear, and like a little girl she scooted her chair right up next to Teo, holding onto his arm and hiding her face. Teresa, Filó said, didn't understand where things were heading. She laughed, tousled the guy's hair and said: you know, my friend, we're serious girls. Teo burst out laughing and the man grabbed Teresa by the thigh, saying, oh I'm sure you're not too serious. She was drunk and I think she liked the way his thick hand felt on her leg. The man pulled her face close, toward the fungus on his neck. She shivered and closed her eyes. His hands moved up her thigh, and she looked like she was enjoying it, remaining soft to his touch. But when he leaned in for a kiss, she screamed. He held her fast and tried to force her. She leapt out of her chair, knocking it to the floor along with their drinks. Teo got between them. Teresa was crying, saying she wanted to go, trembling. Everyone in the bar was watching—other people stood up. Teo pulled the two of them out of the bar, hurried and angry. Teresa wouldn't stop crying and saying, he has a rotten tooth, he has a rotten tooth. The whole town was dark, and they were a long way from the boat. Teresa spat on the ground, still trembling. Teo was trying to hurry them along, saying they couldn't stop.

The man caught up to them, smashed a bottle over Teo's head, and pulled Teresa by the arm. Teo fell, his face covered in blood. Filó ran to help him and didn't see where the man took Teresa. Everything happened so fast, she said. Then they heard Teresa screaming and the man cursing. Teo got up and ran in the direction of the screams. He found Teresa with her dress and underwear torn, and that guy was punching her in the face. They started fighting. The other man had a knife. Teresa was wailing, and had a rock in her hand. Teo grabbed the stone from her and smashed it against the man's hand. That was when Rafa, Helinho, and Neca showed up. Teo kept striking the man with the stone until Rafa and Helinho pulled him off. Then they all made for the boat.

They put a shirt on Teresa. Her legs were bloody and she wouldn't stop crying. When they got to a street with lights, near the docks, they saw that Teo's shirt was stained with blood. He stumbled toward the boat and fell to the ground. There was a doctor on the upper deck who wanted to take your father to the hospital. The captain said no, it was better to get him fixed up right there. They carried Teo to the upper deck. The cut across his stomach was deep and ugly, but it hadn't pierced any organs. They managed to disinfect it and I think the guy sewed him up with a regular needle and thread. He seemed like a good doctor. Teo slept through that night in one of the upper cabins. I stayed beside him in case he needed anything. It was the captain who arranged everything. I could tell he wasn't concerned about the conditions in the hospital at Bom Jesus, or trying to show us any special consideration. He was afraid of some kind of mix-up with the police. Tucking him away on that cot, apart from the other passengers and out of sight to passersby on the docks, it would be easier to get out of there without a hassle.

I don't know, Benjamim, I don't know if the guy died. We never found out. Helinho says Teo was bashing him really hard with that stone—he was crazed. Teresa was scraped up and had bruises all over, her face was swollen. But the blood was from her period. That's why the guy was cussing and started to beat her—not because she resisted, but because she was on the rag. The other girls took care of her.

Teo woke up in the early morning hours asking if Teresa was all right. I said she was. He fell back asleep, groaning, making a noise like he was crying, crying in his sleep. I gave him a little nudge to disrupt his bad dream. He sat up with a jolt and yelled, son of a bitch, son of a bitch, son of a bitch, then fell back on the bed moaning in pain. The cut had re-opened a little, oozing a blood lightened by the dressing on the wound. I wanted to call the doctor but he wouldn't let me. He pressed hard against his stomach and said the pain went away. It was still before dawn when the boat started to whistle, giving the signal that it was about to leave. I don't know how they got going without that missing piece, but we departed while it was still dark in Bom Jesus da Lapa. The noise woke Teo and he couldn't get back to sleep. I think he's dead, he said, I think I killed the son of a bitch. They'll have to find another driver. All the believers, the faithful, the ones fulfilling their promises—they're gonna have to figure something else out. So will I.

Isabel

L ight of my life! Benjamim my boy, son of good fortune, praise the Lord! That was how your grandfather greeted you. You still have that same bright skin you had when you were a boy. Your father didn't bring you to the burial or come himself. After Xavier died, Teodoro only returned after I went to find him.

When he left São Paulo at seventeen, I thought his journey was just a boy's adventure. When you were born two years later, I saw I'd understood nothing, I didn't know what he was getting himself mixed up in. It didn't have to do with any deep political understanding of Brazil or his role in it—as was the case with Henrique, with all those visits to factories, his sudden taste for playing pool in bars on the outskirts of town, his work in the favelas. And it wasn't a hippie thing, which I started to let myself imagine—maybe because of what Flora told me about her experiences and the trips she took with her group, looking for a broader contact with wild nature, both her own and the world's. It wasn't anything like that. At a certain point Teodoro's letters made it seem like he was up to something more along the lines of what his sister Leonor was doing, something related to his music, but without that puritan attitude she had toward her studies. Lenoca, in those days, was on a macrobiotic diet, woke at dawn to practice yoga, spent hours practicing classical piano and avant-garde contemporary music. She was turning sallow and I was afraid that one of those days I might find her levitating. It was a relief when she got into folk music and started studying its origins. It was something more earthy. Teodoro sent her scores of the songs he'd heard and transcribed. I imagined that with his scientific mind, he would end up doing some kind of research like that, maybe something related to cultural anthropology.

The path selected by each of my children was new to me, not only in terms of their professional choices, but also the mishaps and thickets they had to navigate before they could stand on their own two feet. Xavier didn't pay much attention. He talked with them and wasn't surprised by anything. He treated them as equals, competed with them, found it all touching. I didn't have any parameters for how to follow along. I was the one being guided, towed. I returned to adolescence along with each of my kids. I confess that I became curious, maybe even excited, when Flora started sleeping with her boyfriend at home, and when Henrique told me that he'd smoked pot. The fact that I still had to organize dinner, call the cleaner, send the laundry out, dress wounds, balance the checkbook, and, eventually, provide the basics that each of them needed to leave home—because of all that I never became much smarter than any of my kids. I always had common sense, the kind that's linked to survival. Whenever I intuited some kind of larger risk, I channeled the spirit of Dr. Belmiro and tried to act as the judge in the story, to get a little closer, to be a voice not of conservatism, I thought, but of conservation. In the end, life takes care of itself and, whether wounded or dead, almost everyone is saved.

Before Teodoro's trip with his friends on the São Francisco steamer, before his disappearance, his letters could be confusing and, at times, indicated a state of disorientation. But they were the letters of someone who took an interest in the world. Later, when he started writing again, the letters were shorter and more formal—it seemed like he was just fulfilling the basic obligation to stay in touch. Before he went to live in Cipó, he bounced between a few nearby estates. I didn't understand his interest in that kind of life. I never found out about the fight in Bom Jesus da Lapa, or about his illness, just like I didn't find out about his marriage to Elenir, or about your birth, until later. I was led to believe that he was tired and wanted to be left alone. I thought about going to visit him, even against his will. But I was always busy with something: grandchildren being born, obligations at the university—by this point I was chair of the department. And Xavier was sick.

Then Teodoro came back. He was odd, different, a little too mature, almost like an old man. He'd always had an old soul. He was born that way. He was more defensive than the others, more closed-off. It was only after he came back that I realized how much he must have suffered in the years he stayed away. He was tough, and had the body of a manual laborer: broad shoulders, rough hands. You were a joyful child, curious. You got along with the whole family. Teodoro never let you out of his sight. He seemed afraid that one of us might do you some kind of harm.

After Xavier died, I went to Cipó while Teo was still living there. The second time was to bring you, both of you, back here with me. Leonor had gone once during one of her vacations and sent me vague reports, without telling me the whole story. She took Renata and Rodrigo, and the three of them stayed in the Hotel da Serra for a whole month. You went to spend a holiday at her house, too, but I think it was only that one time. Teodoro didn't like to be separated from you. He was so attached. But maybe it was also because you came back from Leonor's with strange new ideas, not from that place. When you were little you liked São Paulo. Henrique never went to Cipó—he never had any patience for your father. The eldest and the baby of the family. But in the end it was thanks to Henrique that I finally managed to get a hold on things.

Haroldo told you about Xavier's crisis, but that's something else entirely—and I'm sure he exaggerated. He's a lawyer—you should always remember that. He's making a case for himself. Maybe he told you a story in which he plays a nice part, and I don't blame him for that. The truth is that in this story, no one can say they did what was right or wrong. Vanity and fantasy aside, the important thing for you to know is that there isn't a history of madness in the family. Not that it would be a problem if there were. But the point is that it's not the case for us. These days, it's fashionable to attribute everything to depression, to bipolar disorder, to genetics. Teodoro definitely went crazy, but the world and the choices a person makes in life can also lead to madness. We have some power over our destinies. You can't reduce everything to genetics.

I smoked my entirely life, I never exercised or went to the gym. I hate all that. I prefer nighttime to daytime, the city to the country, white rice and red meat. I adore refined sugar, thick guava jam, crème brûlée, and I inhale deeply when I smoke, or at least I did. And now it's this. Those are choices, what you do with your life, what I did, what the world did to me. Here I am, full of tubes, dying of cancer, talking to my beloved grandson—a graphic designer in Rio de Janeiro, and probably the author of brilliant slogans and logos that synthesize the most profound human ambitions: victory, action, buy, do, now, always, the colorful emptiness, the portals to hell now flooded by ambient noise and sweet smells. Benjamim, take pity on me, or at least have a little more curiosity about your old grandmother. What are you looking for? What can I possibly still give you? You have a body, color, voice, a life in front of you. There's not much left of me. But what's left is mine. I made it.

Forgive my ill-humored grandstanding. I manage even to take pride in my cancer—it's pathetic. I didn't sleep well, these tubes are uncomfortable, everything hurts. I don't want morphine. I know that if I start taking it I'll never be able to stop. *La vecchiaia è brutta.* That's just it: old age is shit. I wouldn't have done anything differently, but it's shit, it really is. As my father would say, *le mot de Cambronne.* He also said that a whistling girl would make angels cry. That was another time. They did all the same things we did, but the way they talked was different, and that always mattered. I don't mean to be hostile, not to you, my dear. You're right, we should talk, I don't like the distance that came between us. I know I'm the one responsible: you were a child. It wasn't what was right, but it's what was possible. There isn't time for us to become friends, but we can at least distract each other until the end. Your visits do me good, even if I seem grouchy. It's these tubes, not you. "Son of good fortune." I'll admit I never liked that Xavier would greet you like that. It was always clear to me that he also referred to his dead son, the one he had with Elenir. Your grandfather immediately knew who you were. I saw that he recognized it in you. Benjamim, Rachel's son, Jacob's favorite. "Seven years upon the mountainside / Jacob watched the flocks for Rachel's father Laban / He served not the father, but for the lovely daughter / to him was promised as his future bride." Do you remember? Camões. Did you have to study him in school? In our home, everyone knew it by heart. Xavier loved reciting Camões however he remembered it, right or wrong. He did it in the shower, on long car trips. Ah, "son of good fortune," they all died—it's just us left. Now maybe I can get used to that epithet. It suits you—it brings together your goodwill and the radiance in your face.

Nobody has the patience to come and visit, which is fine by me. Everyone has their own life to live, and death is an ugly beast. The hospital is far, there's so much traffic, but insurance doesn't cover a live-in nurse and I don't want to be a burden to anyone. I prefer this anodyne, impersonal space. I can tolerate incompetence if I'm allowed get angry and yell. Here I don't owe anyone any favors. I was Xavier's caregiver right to the very end. Teodoro brought you here and took you back the night before Xavier died. Now it's the eve of death once more: you came and you'll stay, I know it. Then you'll be able to say your goodbyes.

Talking to you in this sea-green room reminds me of many things. I'm able to miss Teodoro without feeling so sad, without ambiguous feelings. The one I really miss is Xavier, his energy. I was relieved when he died. It was a long illness, and I never had the patience for taking care of other people. A sick man is so needy—it's hell. Beyond the eternal separation, there was work, kids, husband. It wasn't a calm goodbye. Missing him only came later, and I think I miss him now more than ever. Xavier drunk, making a racket in the street, the house full of kids. No, I don't feel remorse for not having enjoyed it more, the old "I should have spent more time with my family and stayed with my kids when they were young." No, it's just pure nostalgia. Life is the way it is. I rest easy knowing that I instilled respect for hard work in my children, I taught them to dedicate themselves to knowledge, to books.

We grew up together, and that was beautiful in its own way, too. Anyway, my dear *Mineiro*, let's get to Minas. That's our subject, isn't it?

My first trip to Cipó was in July of '85, a year after Xavier died. Teodoro had already been there for several years, ever since you were born. I was perplexed, absolutely shocked by your living conditions. My first instinct was to grab you both by the arm and take you back to São Paulo right then. That farmworker's shack and the tight little room where you lived were revolting. I'd already reached my limit. Since you were born there, you can't imagine my shock. And here, all you ever knew was my apartment—a more modest lifestyle than what we had before. But you can get an idea of the contrast, starting with the physical contrast I saw in your father's condition. Now, imagine how it was for me, the daughter of Dr. Belmiro and Dona Lurdes, imagine what a shock it was. Even after making it through adolescence with the other three, I wasn't prepared for what I saw. It was utter contempt, an act of aggression on Teodoro's part, without a trace of irony. Today I can even see the humor in it, even though I still don't find it funny. What I mean is that I've managed to craft a gentler narrative, and can at least smile at my bourgeois surprise. At the time it wasn't so easy.

I'd made a reservation at the Hotel da Serra, which was the only one out there. I turned up to see you unannounced. I asked Henrique to come with me, but he refused. I didn't invite Flora because I had some idea of how conservative the environment would be that far into the interior, and was afraid she'd end up causing problems. Lenoca was the only one of them who kept in touch with your father. She'd already gone once, she'd gotten to know the people and the place, and was totally against the idea of me going. So I went by myself.

I could tell that something wasn't right. It wasn't right for me to be so separated from my son and my grandchild. I was afraid of how Teo would react. He hadn't come to his father's burial and our last encounter hadn't gone well.

Well I got there fine, and the place, your beloved Cipó, I admit, was lovely. The hotel was comfortable and decent. I took a nice bath, unpacked my things, took a deep breath, and went out to the plantation. It was a cool and clear afternoon, and everyone I passed along the way was nice, but my heart was lurching. When I got to the farm nobody knew anyone called Teodoro Kremz. Then I saw you playing with some other boys, in the yard in front of the big house. You looked like a gang of monkeys, climbing the trees and rolling around on the ground. When I called your name, you stopped dead in your tracks and stared at me, frightened. Then the peasant woman who'd brought me understood that I was looking for Tito, Beibi's father.

Dona Zefa, who was watching from the verandah, came over to find out what I wanted and greeted me warmly. She offered me a drink, took me to the verandah, and sent a girl to fetch Teodoro from the field. Not knowing how I was going to find him, and envisioning that he would react poorly to my visit, invading his space, I'd brought just one little toy for you and a small gift for the woman who owned the farm—I don't even remember what it was anymore, maybe a hand-embroidered towel. It took more than an hour for Teodoro to arrive, so I had time to talk with Dona Zefa. We even discovered that we had some family connections. She was horrified that Teodoro had never mentioned anything about his family to her. Anyway, we weren't related by blood, but by marriage: a great uncle of hers, I think he was called Pimenta Toledo, married a distant aunt of mine—I think she was my grandmother's second cousin by marriage on her mother's side, the Queriós branch. While we waited for Teodoro I had time to tour the house and meet Dona Zefa's sons, daughters, grandchildren, great-uncle, aunt, mother, and her old and nearly blind nanny, her blue eyes glazed in white, her tiny body bent and black—who knows how many servants they had in that house. I thought they were a sweet family. Everyone was so kind. The house was a bit chaotic, significantly altered from the original—it was divided into the hallways and rooms and nooks that you know so well. I admired the solid architecture. Beautiful, broad floorboards—you can't find those in São Paulo anymore. The braided-straw wainscoting was new to me. It wasn't used on plantations around São Paulo. I thought the little chapel was darling, with those baroque saints, tall candles, and lacy tablecloths, the walls painted blue and pink. But I found it odd for the kitchen to be a stucco addition, just sort of slapped on to the house. Is it still like that? I remember the immense hearth, and those lovely countertops, painted the same red as the wood-burning stove top, and people and kids buzzing around all over the place. It was hard to tell the servants from the family. It wasn't like the coffee plantations I knew as a girl. It was much older, and it emanated vestiges of another kind of power: less ostentatious, perhaps, but heavier, more natural.

The calm and welcoming reception, and Teodoro's delay in arriving, allowed Dona Zefa to recognize me for the lady that I was and still am—not the mother of some ranch hand called Tito. And I, on the other hand, was able to see that they were a close-knit family. This generous introduction both calmed me and afflicted me. On the way to Cipó I'd been haunted by two possibilities: the first was that I'd be poorly received by Teodoro, I was afraid he'd make some kind of scene; the second fear was that I'd be treated poorly by the owners of the plantation, Teodoro's masters. That's "masters" in quotation marks—and it was my own strong term, always in quotes. What kind of awful people could think they were my son's masters? I couldn't swallow it.

It's odd, isn't it? Silly, elitist? All true, and to this day I also find it odd that Fábio, Henrique's son, who works for a multinational drug company, is a manager—or rather, just another employee. Laura, Flora's daughter, is a bank attorney. Rodrigo, Leonor's son, is a marketing intern at a cosmetic brand. And even Renata, poor thing, is the publicist at a publishing company. Maybe I'm crazy, but I can't get used to it. What I mean is, I think it's great they have jobs and make their own money. There's no doubt they're qualified. How many young people their age today still have to depend on their parents, who barely get to retire? Just look at your cousin Guilherme, Flora's son, twenty-something years old and suffering some kind of arrested development. Always out at the bars, sucking money out of Flora that she doesn't even have. So of course I think it's important to work, no matter what kind of work, as long as it's an honest living and doesn't torment the parents. Taking responsibility, it demonstrates persistence, ability, character. But I still find it odd. It's just not right to accept being a cog in a machine, to submit to other people's projects, not develop anything of one's own—to feel the right not to have any ambition or cultivate a greatness of spirit. Yes, because negotiating, battling, resisting, yielding—that's what makes us grow. The problem isn't with being someone's employee, far from it. It's the alienation, the halted construction of a self that serves the world somehow. Growing for the sake of growth means nothing—it doesn't matter if you become a nicer, better person or achieve a high quality of life or any of that nonsense. We grow so that we can accomplish unique and useful works. We have to give back and not be complacent. Work frees parents from their children, from their checkbooks at least, and I realize that's very important. But work for the sake of work never freed anyone. It's more like a prison. At the school, and then at the university, I developed my own work, using my own ideas as my guide. There's such a thing as a collective project—but what kind of projects are there at a bank or at a cosmetics company? Okay, a publishing house is something else and can be noble work. But what sort of participation does a publicist have in any of that? You know what Renata does? She macerates books, draining them of any kind of special difference with the hopes of reaching the sort of people who will only read whatever's put right in front of them, whatever is chewed up and spit down their throats. Can anyone be proud of that kind of journalistic assassination, on a weekly basis? Can you be proud of what you've accomplished at the end of the month if all you did was collaborate on a project that made a bunch of money or sold a bunch of antiwrinkle cream? What does the world gain from any of that? What have you improved? I don't get it. No, I get it—I just don't agree with it.

Those of us who had the privilege of getting the kind of educations we had: we have different obligations than most people, different responsibilities. I think it's great that there's banks for people to use, and industries and services. They make the world work, they give jobs and make products and fortunes. I have nothing against it. It's not a political question, it's a moral one. You can't just be part of the machine—you need to take charge. That's your responsibility. Not for money or power, but because you should do something to give back to your country. We don't have the right to be led around like livestock. If Teodoro were living in the most miserable village in all of Brazil, teaching in a primary school with a leaking roof and not a single desk for the barefoot, crusty-eyed, starving little children to sit at—and for that reason was so poor he had to live in a tiny room off the lands and charity of the local squire—then I'd have been proud of him. But that wasn't what your father was doing.

I feel nauseous, my mouth is dry. But what bothers me the most is that I can't smoke. Old age transforms us. And I'm not talking about senility or anything to do with neurons. It must be a lack of patience. A lifetime of policing our own behavior tires us out, we have nothing to prove to anybody, and we lose all sense of shame. If everyone felt that way, the world would be intolerable—everyone constantly saying whatever's on their mind. But nature is wise: it reserves this pleasure for elders. Maybe it's a mechanism by which the species guides us on toward death—because it's a kind of suicide to take leave of all social conventions.

Benjamim, I want the best for you. It's how I'm able to restrain myself. Not that I have anything bad to say about the family who raised you. My problem isn't with them, like I said: they were lovely, affectionate people. The problem was the relationship your father established with them: this I could not tolerate. I admit that it was the sort of cultural environment that gets on my nerves: one where nothing is clear, everything is complicated and full of obtuse silences. Maybe if my son and grandson weren't stuck in that quicksand, I'd have been able to approach it with academic discernment, or have the curiosity to analyze the rich linguistic heritage in the ways they spoke. But I didn't have the necessary distance from the situation, and anyway, I never had much patience for the sciences. I prefer novels. But my reading glasses are worthless. Tomorrow, before you come, run by a pharmacy and get me some with 3.5 lenses. Every two pages my eyes tire and I get a headache. I can't concentrate.

I'm all over the place, I know. When you start to squirm in the chair like that I realize I'm getting away from myself. With you sitting here in front of me, it's more difficult to remember things than when I'm reminiscing by myself. But the focus should be on Teodoro and not me. And specifically, who Teodoro was to you—Teodoro the father, not the son. The grandfather of your son, your little Antonio. Yes ... What stories will you tell him about your grandfather? Will he be grandpa Tito, grandpa Teo or grandpa Teodoro? There must be so many stories about him from Cipó, stories from the plantation where you were born and raised, stories told and retold by our dear Dona Zefa, recorded and cataloged by your auntie Maristela, her daughter, in that touching museum she worked hard to create, and that she displays with so much pride. It's just a matter of going there and asking about the feats and charms of Tito the ranch hand, Tito the guitarist. But you know very well that Teodoro isn't some fictional character: he's my son, the grandson of my father, the great-grandson of my grandfather, the father of my grandson, the grandfather of my future great-grandson, and to this day I don't understand why he thought he had the right.

I still remember my high school literature classes. And I think what you want isn't a simple tale, some folk story—you want an authored story. In folk tales, the names and places and times aren't important. Every character is a device that makes the story work. That's why these stories can be told again and again and still remain more or less the same. "Rosaflor and the Moor," "Little Red Riding Hood"—it's pop culture. But a short story or a novel is different. It's the words—those exact words—that build a story that will forever remain unique. The characters have names, they develop. The actions happen at a place in time—the story is anchored to a time frame. It's the work of a single person and not the collective work of a people. You came to me because you want to have more than a ranch hand father, a guitarist father, a madman father. I'm all over the place again—maybe that's not the point, or not the only point. I'm the one transforming this into literature. I'll try to keep my head above the flood of memories that wash over me here in this hospital bed, pulling me in every direction. Maybe I'm already senile. It's easy for me to say that genetics and neurons aren't everything, but at the end of the day, biology reigns supreme. I'm old.

Here's the facts: Teodoro came up on the verandah drenched in sweat and greeted everyone, including me, with curt politeness. He brought you with him and told you to ask for my blessing—something you did with exasperating ease. We never did any of that in our family. He never sat down, just held his hat in his hands, in front of his body, like one of the meek and affable farmhands of my youth.

He asked Dona Zefa to excuse us and took me around the farm, and then brought me to his room. In that tiny, dark room, free from the tangle of curious children, the two of us were finally alone, but I didn't know what to say. The first thing that came to me was, "Pull yourself together, boy!" But we'd never talked to each other like that. I'd abandoned that expression, so often uttered when I was a girl, in some forgotten corner of my adolescence—and there was no way of starting to use it now on my son. He was so determined to act out the part of humbly receiving his mother and maintaining a certain distance from me, as though there'd never been any real conflict between us. It disturbed me. There was nothing to argue about, no opportunity to fight, no room to try to understand or even to show simple affection—a caress of the face, or a joke about the austerity of his cloister. It was a man who stood before me—there was nothing left of the boy. Henrique was already a man, too, but he continued to be my son, and therefore was in some ways still a child. There existed within him something of childhood as well as its inverse, the part of him who was the man who'd came to look after his widowed mother. That was Henrique. In Teodoro there was nothing but a hollowness. He was almost a stranger, or worse, an acquaintance.

I asked if he was still composing music and he said no, but he'd learned songs from Cipó and from the singers who came through the area to play. And he would play them, in simplified form, for his friends at parties. Was he still writing? A little, almost nothing. And his drawings? I like to draw with Benjamim, with the children. We sometimes play at drawing and they create beautiful things. Would you like to see some? No, not now, maybe later. And thinking. Was he still thinking? About the livestock, the horses, keeping the bridles and tack in order, polishing the saddles, airing out the saddle blankets, maintaining the fences, vaccinating the animals, separating the pregnant cows from the younger ones, about weeds and grass and rain and droughts? I think about Benjamim, about the hens and the pigs. I think about life, ma'am.

Ma'am, you son of a bitch.

I thanked him for his hospitality and left the same day.

Raul

You do resemble Teo—not in your color, or your hair. His was wavy. It's your way of looking at me, of lowering your face when you listen, that way of smiling without twisting your lips: it brings back things I can't put into words, a certain temperature. I remember things differently when I look at you. After what happened on that trip up the São Francisco, I never heard anything else about him. He didn't write and neither did I. Other people interested me more. Our old group disbanded and I didn't miss it. Whenever we ran into each other, we'd fall back into the same jokes and arguments that were no longer relevant. There was also a kind of insecurity that I didn't have any reason to continue feeling, but around them I felt it.

During one of my breaks from college I went backpacking through Europe with Carmem. I'd never left Brazil before, and it all made me euphoric: the air, the sunlight in Amsterdam that seemed to come from above and below, from the canals, that aquatic light against the crooked houses. We rented bikes and pedaled around all day. I was so happy: that mixture of pure air, civilization, art, and being in love with Carmem. I suddenly wished I could share the experience with Teo. I bought a stack of postcards of Van Gogh, Rembrandt, Vermeer, and wrote daily about my sensations.

I remember that I ended one card in the middle of a word, put a hyphen, and continued my sentence on the next card. I sent them all to Leonor's address because I didn't have his. I wanted her to forward them to Teo in the same way, each on its own. I thought it would be funny for him to get the cards out of order—in those days that kind of idea seemed brilliant to me. Then I forgot about all about it, I forgot Teo, I never even asked Leonor if she'd ended up doing as I asked. It was a capsule filled with the longing for Teo I'd carried.

One day I got a postcard from him. It had a photo of a hotel on the front. I went looking for it just so I could show it to you, and I found it: "Hotel da Serra — Cipó — Minas Gerais." Can you read the writing? "Benjamim was born. He's a strong and beautiful boy." Look at the drawing, it must be you, this fat little baby. It's from February 1980, so you were already a few months old. I hadn't heard that he had a son. At that age, having a friend with a son was something so unreal that I interpreted his note as a metaphor, a way of telling me he was all right again, that he'd found whatever he was seeking. Of course I remembered the conversation he'd had with Xavier about his father's dead son, Benjamim. It stuck with me. So I thought he was writing to tell me that he'd made peace with his father or something, and that maybe he'd be going home soon. I didn't write back. I put the postcard in my desk so that I wouldn't forget to reply. One day passed, then two, the three months had gone by and the whole thing started to feel weird. I didn't have anything to say to him. I didn't know this new Teodoro, and didn't want to. I put the postcard in a box with other keepsakes.

Then he turned up in São Paulo to visit his sick father. You were already walking. I went to your grandparents' house to see him. It felt like years since I'd been there, but it hadn't really been very long. Teo took off at the end of '77 and came back with you in '81 or '82. So it was five years max. There was no life left in the place, just a feeling of abandonment. Your grandfather was lying on the sofa, very pale and thin. The old furniture was stained and torn; the windows let a draft in. But I don't know how to explain exactly what it was. The house had always been a little nuts, but it was cheerful, bustling, and even though the furniture was always getting wobblier and then disappearing, my memory was of a clean and pleasant house. Maybe Graça, their longtime maid, had finally retired, with money getting tight as Xavier's illness depleted whatever was left of the inheritance. I don't know how to explain it. Maybe to someone who'd never been there before, the house would've looked a little old and worn out, and not the catastrophe I saw.

It wasn't just the passage of time, and maybe that had nothing to do with it. Come to think, it was the way time had altered my way of seeing things. I saw the mechanisms that had sustained that family—when they ceased to function they were revealed to me. The pulleys were loose, the motor was hesitating. Noticing their existence rendered the mechanisms banal.

Helinho, Rafa, Leonor and the piano, your grandmother, your grandfather, Teo, the avocado tree in the garden, the big dining room table—it was all there, only five years had passed. Your grandmother must've been around fifty, she's about my mother's age. She was a little older than I am now, but what I saw was an old woman. To my childish imagination she was a pretty woman with long legs who wore unusual clothes. But that day I saw a sallow, tired woman. Xavier, always large and commanding, a man with a long gait who gave firm hugs—he was still effusive, but weak. He was so happy to see you all there, pleased with our visit. Xavier knew how to make us feel loved. He greeted me with such a sincere laugh. It was touching. He had some kind of problem with his throat, aside from his lung, so he could only whisper and his voice came out choppy. He was yellow, I don't know if he had cirrhosis as well, or something else going on with his liver. He was a sick man. He wanted to get up and walk around, talk to everyone, play with you, and he was annoyed that he couldn't. He asked your grandmother to do this and that, go and get things for him, make lunch, bring him a beer. He desired the movements he could no longer perform himself, so he made everyone around him keep moving. I went to help Isabel make sandwiches.

Teo had arrived two days earlier. Isabel was really suffering. I'd never seen her afraid before. As we made the sandwiches, she told me that she'd thoroughly cleaned Teo's room. She sent the bedside lamp out to be fixed, washed the comforter, organized everything in the closets and on the shelves—normal things, but for her, housework was not a normal activity. She told me how she felt in the days leading up to his return. She told me that she made up Henrique's room for you, and put a rail on the bed so you wouldn't fall out. At Xavier's insistence, she'd bought some new toys and had sent the old stuffed animals out to be washed. She found the old blocks and toy cars from our model city, cleaned up what she could still salvage, and put them in a new box in a corner of the room.

Teodoro had come by bus. He arrived tired, and I imagine he must have been just as surprised as I was by the state of his parents' house. For Isabel the shock was mutual. She told me that Teo looked like a migrant worker who'd just blown into São Paulo. Much stronger and browner than when he'd left, dusty, wearing boots without socks, carrying a few bags and you, Benjamim, with clothes that barely fit you, your grandmother said, your little belly poking out from under a T-shirt that was too small for you. She described all this to me and then let out a sad laugh, with tears in her eyes. Teodoro was glad to be back, visiting his parents, shooting the shit.

"There were a lot of hugs and kisses. I was dying to see him. Benjamim is such an adorable little boy—lively, clever, so handsome and articulate. We had breakfast, the two of them were starving. Everything was fine." She leaned against the kitchen sink and, clenching the breadknife in her fist, beat the marble countertop, saying to herself, "Why does he have to be so hard on me, why?" I didn't know what to do—how could I console the great Isabel? It was awkward. I bowed my head and silence filled the kitchen. I went to get the ham and cheese and noticed an absence above the fridge: Graça's ever-present cake was no longer there. That void above the refrigerator and most importantly, that look in Isabel's eyes: they marked the end of a youth spent in that house.

Teodoro and his mother kept their distance from each other. He dragged a mattress into his room so that you could sleep near him, and tossed his clothes into the closets and on the floor. He woke up very early and made a ton of noise, ate with his elbows on the table, and hunched over his plate with his mouth open. He wanted his coffee brewed with a cloth filter and sweetened in a pot, he used coconut soap to clean your clothes in the washtub, complained about the way the city smelled of gasoline, he skipped meals and wandered off when Isabel was playing with you—anything he could do to signal distance from his mother. Isabel had never been a housewife, her husband's illness required the kind of caretaking she couldn't perform and didn't enjoy. A lack of money left her without a regular maid, and now she was stuck with her slovenly son and a small child. Outside the house, Teo was a gentle man, very different from the one who left us in Petrolina.

The last time we'd seen each other was toward the end of the riverboat trip up the São Francisco. Two days after the fight in Bom Jesus we docked in Petrolina. Teo had a fever. The doctor said it was normal, prescribed a few pills and instructed him how to treat the cut. We stayed in a hostel that was basically some family's home. They made a wonderful breakfast for us: grilled banana, cassava with butter and mash. The lady who ran the place took Teo under her wing and cared for him while the rest of us explored the town. The plan was to stay two days in Petrolina and then continue by bus to Marechal Deodoro, in Alagoas, and spend the rest of our holiday in a house some friends rented near there. Since your father was hurt, we decided to wait until he got better. Teresa had already split. As soon as we got off the boat, she caught a bus to Recife and flew home to São Paulo. She wanted to be at home with her mom. We didn't talk about what happened. Teo kept quiet and Filó avoided him. On the third day in Petrolina, after we got back to the hostel, Dona Lisete was sobbing. She said he left a note.

"Raul, it's like this. I liked killing that pig. I could end up a vigilante. Billy the Kid, remember? But I still haven't found my Pat Garrett and what I want is to be old and fat, like Hoss from *Bonanza*. Playing tourist is a drag. I killed a guy. It's fucked, man. I'm not cut out for going around as part of a group. It's not fun anymore. Nobody's gonna miss that guy, and nobody will miss me, either. Everyone has to go his own way in life. Say hi to my folks. —Teodoro The Old."

And after that I never heard from him. I moved on with my life.

Teo had been my best friend. There were years when I lived more at his parents' house than I did at mine. And then, from one minute to the next, it didn't matter anymore. I tuned it out. When I remembered him, like I did in Amsterdam, it always had to do with some kind of juvenile excitement and joy, entirely separate from thought, and almost separate from memory. It was more of a sensation than a memory, something that just came over me. If I stopped to think about him, I felt nothing.

That first time he came back to São Paulo, with you on his shoulders, he told me a little about your mother. We'd gone out a few times to talk, in the morning or afternoon, but never at night, because he didn't want to be away from you. He was a strict father: there was mealtime, bedtime, no TV, no junk food. You were a good boy and happily went along with his tough love. We went to the zoo, to Ibirapuera Park, to Butantã. Teo said he'd gotten married. He said your mother was beautiful, a cheerful and competent doctor who'd just arrived in the town where he was hospitalized. Your father had a definite weakness for older women. It had already happened once with a teacher from school. And the way he'd left Dona Lisete so disconsolate at that hostel in Petrolina—it gives you an idea of how he acted. But aside from that, your mother really must have been someone special, because Teo had never really connected with a woman before. What I saw in all those liaisons with older women, most of them married, was Teo's way of avoiding any kind of commitment. With your mother it was different. He told me that he wanted to "build a family," put down roots, not just in one place, but in the world, into a woman. He told me he was seized by the urgent need to settle down. That's the kind of phrase your father would use: "the urgent need to settle down."

I never had that ability. I'm a ghostwriter, a man who inhabits the ideas and lives of others. My memory substitutes my lack of imagination. I'm the type who goes around with a notebook, stealing phrases I lift from the checkout line, from balconies and parties. The other day a friend of mine wrote a song and asked me to write lyrics for it. He wanted it to be something related to madness and medications. We talked it over for quite a while and a few days later I sent him the lyrics. He said it was good, but I could tell he didn't like it. I pressed him on it, and he admitted it was true—he said the problem was that I'd written exactly what he'd asked for. You see what I mean? I write exactly what they ask for. And what are you asking for? For me to talk about Teo. And that means talking about someone better who got left behind while I moved ahead.

When it comes to your mother, all I can tell you about is Teo's Leninha. When he started to talk about her he stopped, got quiet, and seemed to forget I was there. Then he came back to himself and told me about the house they shared, about her doctor's uniform. For the first time in our lives, we talked about love.

That was more than twenty years ago. I'd remembered what he'd said, but not that atmosphere between us. It was both touching and awkward. Teo, the one who was open, romantic, so exposed—he wasn't just different, but a bit damaged as well. Teo had always been attentive to language and styles. He was sort of a poseur, you know? He was pop, then he was alternative, cool, macho. He was never really the thing itself, almost like he was too intelligent to surrender his critical distance from it. And when he spoke about your mother he couldn't find the right words. The more lyric and romantic he got, the farther he was from his own language, and the more sincere his clichés. He couldn't describe your mother in his own words—he'd never learned how. He needed the sort of words that were always forbidden between us, and I guess they were forbidden in his own mind, too. So he had to string together borrowed words. It was sincere and, at the same time commonplace, becoming just another of his stories. Only this time, repeating his father, he told the story of your birth: the past once more denied, erased. He was sick when he met your mother. Delirious, even.

"When I opened my eyes, I was in a hospital ward. One guy had a hacking cough, another was moaning. Footsteps shook the bed and echoed across the room, there were whispers in the pink sunset light. I tried to get up and I couldn't. I had no strength and there was a tube sticking out my arm. My lips were chapped and I was sweating, the sheet drenched against my skin. Then I saw the hips, the belly, and the breasts of a woman through the contours of her white dress as she approached, a glass of water in hand. I took the hand and the cup, the water was so good and the hand so cool. Its soft fingers straightened my wet hair and I looked up at her face. Raul, those tranquil eyes, the laugh on her closed mouth, the color of her skin. I found her. That's what I thought: I found my life. 'My eyes saw and my heart understood'—that old line was just what happened to me in that instant. I felt even weaker, a rag doll, a pathetic bird flying through the dust of what had been, until then, my wanderings."

During the month that he was hospitalized, Leninha came every day. He only got better after she accepted his marriage proposal.

"I was a miserable stray: no mother, no father, no direction. She took pity on me, orphaned there at the hospital. As days went on her watch, I became a man again. But she didn't stop coming to stay with me. The two of us would sit together looking out at the twilight.

"There came a time when I began to recognize her foot-steps on the other side of the room—I'd get hard and my heart would start thumping. After finishing a round of checkups on all her patients, she'd come over to my rickety bed, take my pulse, and find it strange that my heart rate never matched the numbers marked by the morning nurse. She'd put two warm fingers against my frozen wrist and smile, intrigued. Those dark lips parting and her vivid red tongue pumped the blood through my arteries even faster, sometimes skipping beats. We said almost nothing to each other."

Teo stopped, caught his breath. He was watching you play on the edge of the lake and said that your color was the same as your mother's, that you had the same gentle look in your eyes.

"I was afraid of getting better and then losing that corner of her heart I felt I'd already conquered. At the same time, I had an urge to get up, walk around, get to work, to be a man for her. It was all so important that I was afraid of messing up. Leninha was so complete, why would she need a boy like me, a boy who could offer her nothing? I didn't have a job, I was nobody, I was barely even sick.

"I was getting nervous. Every conversation was excruciating, and after she left I always felt like an idiot. I'd get angry thinking back over everything I said. Just forget it, forget it, forget it, I told myself. But that didn't help. I'd let myself think that she touched my face and took my pulse with a different gesture, a caress. But it was nothing, it was just my anxiety transforming everything. Nothing about it was special for her. I started to watch the way she attended to the old lady near the door, the ugly man with the cough in the middle of the room. Always with the same delicate languor. The languor with which my turn drew near. And when it came, I could only ever say stupid things. Every day I got crabbier about my words. I even thought maybe I should jump out of bed and fuck one of the nurses on her beloved ward, in front of all the old and dying patients, just to hurt her, to prove that I didn't need her, that I didn't want her, that I'd never loved her. And that would prove once and for all that I was a worthless cad. Any chance I had with her would be blown, and I'd be free again. I tried to be ironic during our conversations, but she always disarmed me. I couldn't find a way to be bad anymore.

"One day I got the courage to look at her, to look at her and tell her. And she already knew. She knew me since before I was born—that was what she said when I refused to leave the hospital. I realized it was the immense longing I felt for her that compelled me to wander and wander and kill and almost die. She said yes."

The two of them married in front of the little altar that Leninha kept at home. No priest, no judge, he'd told me in a soft voice—just an affair between Teodoro, Leninha, and the universe. Teodoro went to live with her and then started working. Soon after she got pregnant. She knew it was a risk at her age, especially considering the precarious condition of the little town hospital. Teodoro believed they were living under some kind of heavenly protection that would ward off all evil. You could have come to São Paulo, I told him, and asked your parents for help. "I couldn't, Raul," Teo told me, "I didn't have a mother or father anymore. I didn't have a past. My life had just started there and then. Looking for help in a past that was no longer mine would've contaminated our son—he was ours but didn't belong to us, the fruit of some higher power we had no right to interfere with—only accept and give our blessing."

This unbelievably esoteric Teo told me that while you were growing in your mother's belly and while she, in the evening, sat in an armchair sewing and embroidering clothes for you, he would play the guitar and "try to understand the joy that Leninha felt in throwing herself into this unknown world to make way for a child of mine."

"We talked about birth and death as though they were the same thing. Leninha said if God had chosen her to be the mother of my son, she was happy with that. He would be born healthy and strong, without a doubt, well made for the land that would be his home. And on that land he would know how to make beautiful things grow, the way that only children born of love are able to do."

It was such a strange conversation: this wasn't the Teo I knew. He seemed to be afraid of thinking for himself, of suffering. He sounded like a diehard believer repeating the sermons of his mediocre pastor. During that conversation I understood why he went to become a ranch hand, why it made some kind of sense. I can't say if it was your mother's death or just the fact that he met her, but his encounter with her did something to his head. Thinking about Teo's words, knowing what I know today, they both seem to have figured out who the other one was and decided to repeat history regardless. For Teodoro, I'm certain the marriage had something incestuous about it. Sleeping with your father's woman: can anyone stand it without gouging his eyes out and being condemned to wander? She had to die, they both knew that— one of them would have to die and this time it wouldn't be the baby. It's this violence that I finally understand.

As far as your mother is concerned, I don't know. I never

met her. Teo nearly transformed her into a saint, the mother who birthed his true destiny. I don't know why, Benjamim, you're her son, you're much more determined than your father ever was. I see it, but maybe it's wrong to talk about a woman I never met. Xavier and your father used an almost mystical vocabulary when they spoke about her, about what their lives were like with her. Maybe not for Xavier, but with Teo I can't stop thinking there must've been something cruel about your mother, about the way that she deliberately let herself die giving birth to Xavier's grandson.

Learning that Leninha was the same person as the mother of Xavier's first child—it helped clarify the story Teo told me in the park that Sunday, and the strange shape he was in.

He said your mother wanted you to be called Ismael. He showed me a tiny leather bag, sewn shut on each side, and containing something hard inside. It looked like something the indigenous people use, an amulet. She'd embroidered the leather with little colored seeds, spelling out the name Ismael, two birds, and a fish. He said that Leninha was certain her child would be a boy, and she wanted him to be called Ismael. The birds were the two of them, and also the Holy Spirit. And the fish, a symbol of renewed life, "because she was Catholic, but didn't like the imagery of the crucifix, she thought that God protected us and that He showed us our way in life through the words of his Son, and not through His death, that in the Resurrection we would always be as we were in our greatest moments of love." Teodoro told me all this laughing, almost reciting in the tone of a children's song, in the tone of someone who doesn't believe what he says but still finds it beautiful.

"Ismael was the son Abraham had with his slave, and he was Abraham's heir until his wife, Sarah, finally had a son and

Ismael had to flee with his mother and from Sarah's jealous wrath. The legend says that Mohammad and the Muslims are descendants of Ismael. Leninha wanted our son to be called Ismael. She wanted our son to be a new beginning, a man who strays from the flock." She died and Teodoro said that you were like a renewed beginning for the one who died and got left behind, the rebirth of a dream that hadn't come true, a father's vision that was only now made real.

He told us that a nurse from the hospital, a friend of Leninha's, wanted to help him with the little boy and that he left you with her for a few days. After your mother's burial, he was home alone. He'd wake up, use the bathroom, take a bath, and dry himself in the sun, pacing the hot cement under the empty clothesline. Then he'd go back to bed. He said he didn't cry, didn't pray, didn't get said. He ate bananas from the bunches he plucked from the banana tree in the back. Sometimes he'd wake up in the early morning, while it was still dark, open his bedroom window, and strum his guitar. He wondered if Leninha liked the Beatles and the Rolling Stones, if she'd ever heard the Novos Baianos. They'd never spoken about it. Neither of them had a past. Maybe because Xavier was there, behind it all, drawing them in, haunting them. Or maybe there was no reason, that's just the way it was, Teo told me that day in the park.

"The important thing is to have this love inside me and my son. It makes no difference whether she's alive or dead. After she died I missed seeing the shape of her face, feeling her soft breasts, tasting her salty neck. I liked the scent of her sweat. I didn't miss her—I missed her voice and the sound of her rocking chair, which moved to the rhythm of her fingers as she knit. I didn't miss her. I don't miss her. At home, after she died, I undressed and sat on the hot cement under the clothesline and stayed there. I had a child and I had love. Some of my clothes were hanging there to dry with Leninha's. Then came wind, sun, and rain, and the clothes no longer held our smells. It was good to be alone with just my body: muscles, bones, and skin. Later I took my clothes down from the line and got dressed. They smelled like the sun, the fabric parched and crisp. It felt hot on my skin, the pants scraped my leg, the shirt scratched my belly, and I felt like I'd returned to the world."

He felt more like a man for having a male child, and for being the widower of his father's beloved. Teo went and got you from the nurse's house, thanked her and took off. Teo said that the two of you would be welcomed wherever you went because he was strong and you were little. On the afternoon of the second day, he decided to stay on the farm where you were raised. He became a ranch hand.

You were just a little boy that day, playing in the park. You ran up to him at one point, trying to show him something. He widened his eyes, lifted his eyebrows, and with a jump he took off running, chasing you, pretending to be a ferocious wolf who wanted to catch and eat a brave little boy. You turned and made a courageous face, raising a gun made of two fingers and a thumb and firing straight into Teo's forehead. He fell with his arms wide open, his tongue sticking out of his mouth, exaggerating his death. You were so cute: you marched in circles around him and in your little voice you started to sing a song that he and I used to sing when we were young. He opened his eyes and sang along: "We're the hunters, and nothing scares us! We shoot a thousand bullets a day, and kill innumerable beasts! We patrol the whole forest, through valleys and over the mountains! We hunt the spotted jaguar, cavies, armadillos, and cotias!" I'd never seen him so happy. You say that in Cipó he was always that way, always playing pretend and telling stories. But it was new and strange to me. Part of the story was missing.

Haroldo

Duty calls, my boy! Even though I'm retired my services are still in high demand. Whenever she wanted to get one of her kids' attention, Dona Silvia would quote her grandfather, saying, "Man is captive to his duties." And Xavier would object, and say, "As I am captive to my pleasures!" And that's pretty much how it was: his great-grandfather left them big farms and had a hand in the construction of the railway system. His father built hospitals, made a name for himself in academia. And my friend Xavier? He wrote articles, translated and wrote incomprehensible novels long since destroyed by mold and moths, put on plays that were gone with the wind. In certain recondite circles he might still be remembered, but not for much longer. He never had the courage to be a real artist, and that's the truth.

São Paulo is unforgiving: it takes what you never accomplished and rubs it in your face so that your life just gets worse and worse, and proof of your failures keep getting more obvious: You never made it! You never came close! That's what the blinking neon lights on Avenida Paulista always seem to say. Xavier felt those blows and died young. He couldn't stand any confirmation of his failures once he was left with an empty nest, that big house without any kids. They were the only lasting thing he'd ever done. But anyway, I'm sure it's only in São Paulo where that's remarkable, at least if we're talking in terms of Brazil—and there's no use of thinking about the rest of the world because then we'd be entering the realm of abstraction.

No matter how hard you work in Rio de Janeiro, Belo Horizonte, or Porto Alegre, you won't get very far unless you pass through São Paulo from time to time. Because the decisions are all made here, this is where the money is, where ideas are exchanged. It's where the rubber hits the road, where you work a lot and make a name that will stand the test of time. Here it's our work—and not the kids we have or the lives we lead—that matters in the end. From up here you look down and see the city. Our first office was over there, in the city center. It's been fifteen years since we moved here, to Avenida Paulista. Now everybody wants to move again, over there off Avenida Berrini. I'm glad I'm almost retired. What would I do down there, with that river and those cars and trucks and without this view of the horizon? But that's the new frontier. The problem is that we're always burning out the old ones, leaving scorched earth.

I was born in the Campos Elíseos, and the first office was in Líbero Badaró. They were decent neighborhoods, even somewhat chic. Paulista might last, but I get the impression that once we all start to move out, the rearguard will be in retreat and decay will take over. I'd like it if we could resist for a little longer, show a little more gallantry and organization to that huge, amorphous, hungry, and jaundiced mass that's constantly nipping at our heels. From up here I can look back downtown and see what's left of what we built: shabby brown ruins. Our footprints are already worn away. All that's left are dirty ruins, human ruins. They call them street dwellers. They're poor wretches, but the correct term is urban invaders. They salt the earth on which they walk. The violence of their misery sterilizes their surroundings. And when that happens, all that's produced are more children, nothing else. I'd like to resist from right here, at the top of this spire. But barbarism is cunning. The avenue is already filthy, the sidewalks are cracked, the walls covered in graffiti. I don't like it. Nobody likes walking down a street filled with beggars and families sprawled out on the ground with mattresses, filthy blankets, and dogs, all mixed in with the street vendors. Even the pedestrians are getting uglier. But down by the river, I get the chills when I see the streets so clean and vacant. Huge buildings, recessed buildings, closed off from the street. Cars and more cars—you have to get in through garages, underground passageways, elevators and brushed-steel doors, double-paned windows, green and gray. Glass soldered shut to protect against the noise and the exhaust, against suicide. We abdicate the streets and isolate ourselves, hunted into dark corners. The roles are inverted: in this city, we're the rats.

Around here, even if we're halfway down the road to barbarism, I can still walk from one place to another. I can feel the work getting done in the rushing of office pageboys, in the animated conversations of the young men in ties, in the elegance of the young ladies who hold down the offices. Around here people still walk—although I realize it's with less pleasure and more alarm every day. That's why I prefer the country club. If I actually knew how to use a computer and understood the Internet, I could come here less. But that won't happen in this life.

Xavier, if he were alive, would certainly chuckle at my technological incompetence. He was always plugged into the latest gadgets and had an easy time learning new things. He was a tinkerer—the kind of guy who could repair a watch and rewire a light socket. If he were examined today, he'd probably be diagnosed with something like manic depression. But back then, when he was at the rest home, I don't know if they ever put a name to his crisis. The truth is that his entire life was filled with ups and downs. I already told you, I didn't spend much time with your grandparents after I got back from Europe. But even though I didn't go to their house, I met up with Xavier from time to time over the years, right up until his death. My ex-wife didn't get along with Isabel: they had different ideas about how to raise children, how to keep house. They never fought, but she was critical and jealous of Isabel. So once or twice a year I'd go out to dinner with Xavier, or meet him to catch up over drinks. It had to be when he was on the upswing or else he'd never leave the house. He never got treated for it—he thought that life was made up of cycles and that there was nothing pathological about it. During his periods of depression he wanted silence and stillness. He'd lock himself in his office, writing whatever the newspaper paid him to write, and spend the rest of his time reading and watching TV. He told me that the strategy he'd devised for getting out of these depressive states was studying a new author or learning to read another language. That was his healing process and as far as I could tell it worked rather well. By the time he died, he was able to read and translate not only a few common languages—English, German, French, Spanish, Italian—and the classics, Latin and Greek, but also Arabic, Hungarian, Russian, and Sanskrit. Maybe he didn't exactly master every single one of them, but I think he had more than a basic proficiency in each.

My meetings with Xavier were always stimulating. I'd get back in touch with feelings that were dear to me, things my day-to-day lifestyle prevented me from experiencing. Xavier's informality, his lack of any filter—they revived those uncompromising feelings of youth. And then there was his impressive knowledge of literature, theater, film. Maybe it wasn't all that impressive. But for somebody like me, someone who doesn't have time for novels anymore—well, it was great. It recalibrated my balance. I promised myself I'd read more, see more movies, and sometimes after these meetings I actually followed through for a while. Xavier was like an escape valve for me: our conversations were stimulating because they were useless. With him, I enjoyed wasting time—unlike those endless Sundays with family and friends around somebody's pool, a sort of "leisure" that deeply annoys me. I think that he liked our meetings, too. He asked me things about the business transactions that I'd supervised, about the details of cases he'd seen reported in the newspapers. He still thought like a lawyer, he had a real nose for it, and the intellectual culture of São Francisco never left him. More than once I invited him to take part in a case, especially toward the end, when I realized he was going through serious financial difficulties. I didn't do it out of pity, but because I knew he'd be useful to me. I thought he was so hard up that he'd just get over that stubbornness of his. And I think on one occasion, he was actually on the fence about it. But then he figured out some other way of resolving his financial problems and I didn't try to insist.

He was curious about every type of work, all human activity and occupation—the big businessmen, the thunderous bankruptcies, the financial backers behind various economic and diplomatic negotiations between countries. We also talked quite a bit about history and war, the origins of peoples and languages. It was a rational if somewhat delirious topic. He complained that characters in Brazilian literature were always public servants, intellectuals, artists, prostitutes, and migrant workers, with the occasional businessman—but never industrialists, bankers, or successful executives. Xavier said that tedium, anguish, and creativity weren't exclusive to certain professions.

So it wasn't any kind of disgust for business or a distaste for success that prevented him from making money. I even got to thinking that maybe it was just laziness, or an inability to be systematic and organized. But whenever he told me about his plays, or about any of the other projects he was working on simultaneously, I saw that he actually did have an organized mind.

His publishing company for cheap paperbacks was successful, and he even made some money off it. But that didn't last long, and the only reason it wasn't a bigger failure was that Isabel managed to get her hands on some money that allowed them to close it down properly. After it went under, he threw in the towel, for good, on any business ventures that involved financial risk. And not only financial risks. They were social risks, too. I helped him deal with his creditors and we met more regularly during that time. He was really shaken up by the bankruptcy. Even with his rebellious, alternative style, he was ashamed to have his name dragged through the mud—a scandal. What bothered him the most was hearing his friends place the blame for the company's failure on a lack of culture in Brazil, on public indifference to high literature, the dearth of state funds for the arts. He flew into a fit of rage whenever someone tried to mount a defense predicated on the very mediocrity he tried to remedy.

Your grandfather was a hard-nosed, radical liberal—he knew that the fault was entirely due to his incompetence for basic business management. It had nothing to do with public indifference or the quality of his wares, and everything to do with his inability to strike a balance between losses and gains, supply and demand. It made him feel stupid, mentally deficient—with Xavier, everything was grandiose. He saw his name and his family reputation soiled for eternity, defiled in every public square in the entire universe. His sons would never again be able to walk with their heads upright; his daughters would be denied decent marriages and would have to content themselves with sterile spinsterhood. To his wife, poor Isabel, would fall the burden having a profligate husband, incapable of honoring his debts or his word. He played this character for about a year: the dishonored and stupid Xavier, a pariah among pariahs, the loafer who'd dissipated the inheritance of all his father's hard work. By the end of the year we'd managed to cancel all the debts, close down the business, and donate the rest of the stock of books, which at some point during that dark year Xavier had locked in the wet basement of their house. More than half the books were eaten away by mold and worms. God knows where the other half ended up. With the whole thing resolved, and his eternal dishonor concluded, Xavier returned to his regular myriad activities, without ever daring to hope for another success.

I believe it was fear that drove Xavier out of the business world—and out of the world, I suppose. Fear of taking this city by the horns and showing it who's boss. São Paulo doesn't accept niceties. But he wouldn't tolerate another failure, or worse, being seen as average. He opted instead for intermittence, for happenings, for expression—something I started to understand when I saw his family life, the way he raised his kids. The children, to Xavier, filled the gap left by the great work he left unrealized. I might be wrong, because although our lives intersected many times over the years, our spheres were in other ways worlds apart.

Sometimes I'd talk to him about problems I was having at home, difficulties with Fernanda and her strict outlook on how a family should be. At first I thought it was a natural part of the maternal process, her overprotective mothering, her fears of all kinds, her stunted moral sense. But it kept gnawing at me, and I realized that she was trying to build a shield of armor around the family, more closed off every day. Fernanda made me feel dirty when I came home—it was pathological, exasperating. The world outside the house became something sinister and wrong. She hadn't always been that way. I think the degradation in the quality of life in São Paulo turned her into a frightened and aggressive person. I got used to it in time, and between the two of us we maintained an implicit list of things we weren't going to talk about. Her love for the children and the way she kept the house, along with my career, gave me all the support I needed. I was always grateful to her for that. The problem is that gratitude doesn't fill your belly, if you know what I mean.

Talking to Xavier, I got the feeling that his family was entirely different. He even told me about a few of his affairs, and I got the sense that Isabel knew and didn't care. She was good natured, and accepted men for what they were. I was always afraid that Fernanda would find out about my escapades. That made them more exciting, but at the same time it was a drag. I didn't want to hurt her, and always did what I could to preserve our marriage. In this respect, Xavier seemed to be more the master of his own life. He never once told me about a problem with his wife, with his kids, or anything to do with their home life. His news was always stimulating.

I imagine it was rather hard on him when his youngest

son took off like that. He'd placed so much faith in the two younger ones. Xavier was the kind of person who needed to be surrounded by young people—at work, in the bar, in bed. He was always like that. He said he needed to recharge constantly. I don't mean that he remained adolescent in any way, or that he needed the kind of gushing, enthusiastic praise that only the young are capable of offering. I think it had more to do with the constant acceleration of his mind, and his attachment to beauty. He remained young, in fact, for longer than the rest of us. After Teo took off, which was about the time his oldest son started his career—I think the empty nest tied a knot in his brain. He finally saw that he'd gotten older. And from one minute to the next, he'd become an old man. A fifty-something-year-old guy who up and decides he's old. Well, he started playing the part. In our discussions, he started to talk about the importance of setting up a retirement fund, he regretted not having saved enough to help his kids buy cars and houses, enough to get started on their own.

At the same time, he was annoyed that his eldest son had concerns about the salary at his new job, and was already thinking about his health and retirement plans—that he had to submit to the routine of a mediocre public functionary just so he could save the money he needed to get married. When the young man started participating openly in the protests, Xavier thought it was just something stupid. And when his generosity—because Henrique is a generous person—and his uncertainty carried him into the realm of public service, Xavier thought he was lowering himself. Xavier's contradictory expectations must have been something like magnetic south, a perpetual point of disorientation for his children. And I saw the terrible anguish it caused him. Xavier was irresponsible around the house, too: delightful to friends and lovers, devastating to his children, parasitic to his wife. And I should know. I saw enough, let me tell you—I don't use these words lightly. If he'd at least been brilliant, or wise, his kids would have learned something that might have balanced out his ambiguous demands. He didn't seem to realize, for example, that he never had to submit to the logic of work and routine in his youth, yet was able to start his own family by burning through two inheritances, his and Isabel's. But no, he'd say that what his eldest son lacked was nerve.

But not your father. He was to be the legitimate heir. Xavier wanted Teo to repeat exactly what he'd done when we went to Europe together. As though he'd done such amazing things there. I did my master's in Paris after the war. The city was screwed up, schizophrenic. He lived for the nightlife, wandering the bars, discovering a new theater. I guess in some sense he was doing a master's, too. He stayed only a year and came back to Brazil before me. After his youngest son left home, he started talking about Paris again, and about the period of madness that followed the death of his firstborn—his catastrophic state when he arrived in Paris and how it made him identify with the broken city. But it was only after your father went off to Minas that Xavier started talking about Elenir once more.

When Benjamim died, during that whole period of mourning at home, in the asylum, and then in Paris—he never uttered a word about Elenir's disappearance. He'd talk about his little angel, the love of his life, the dream house she created, where they lived in uninterrupted ecstasy, and about their son's room, the birds on the wall, the curtain with a hem embroidered with tiny daisies, about the birth, the child, the hospital, the death. Elenir dissolved into that enchanted interlude as though she'd died along with the child. I don't know why, but it was only after your father went to Minas that he started to speak in terms of blame and abandonment.

I'd taken a shine to Elenir. She was solid and intelligent, a sweet girl. They'd had their son at the São Paulo maternity hospital. The obstetrician was a friend of your great-grand-father's. I think I was the only friend they'd told, maybe because I had a car and Xavier had forgotten to bring the suitcase he'd packed with clothes for the baby. I picked him up at the hospital and we went together to his house to get the things he'd forgotten. It was a long and difficult delivery. Elenir was too young, her body not fully formed. She went into labor, her water broke, but she wasn't sufficiently dilated. Xavier wanted to supervise everything. He fought with the nurses and the doctors, demanding that they take her to the delivery room. When I first got there, Elenir was trying to keep him busy just so he'd stop stressing everyone out. She asked him to fluff her pillow, cool her forehead with a wet handkerchief, get up and close the window a bit, get back up and open it, then get her a glass of water. She told stories of other drawn-out deliveries that turned out fine, then changed the subject. She was doing it all just to distract him, but he'd inevitably start back up with his disruptive agitation.

She looked at me with relief when I came into the room. She called me over and asked me to take her husband some-where and stall him for as long as possible before returning. Xavier was trying to give me the key to their house so that he could stay there and look after of his wife while I went to fetch their suitcase. Then Elenir had a set of contractions. She couldn't talk, her face tightened. Suffering was visible in every single one of that girl's pores. She gritted her teeth and concentrated on her breathing, panting like a wounded animal. Xavier became agitated and demanded the doctors' attention, as though his wife's condition were the result of some kind of medical error and not the natural labors of birth. When the wave of contractions had passed, she asked if he could please go with me, because she forgot to pack this and that and the other thing, stuff that only Xavier would be able to find. When I left the room, she gave me a such a charming conspiratorial wink, almost childlike—I could barely believe she was in the midst of all that pain. That was Elenir: no ostentation whatsoever, minding my friend's eccentricities with kindness and understanding. I don't think anything in the world would have intimidated that girl. I felt an immense tenderness for her. Disheveled and sweating, with her face blotched from so much strain—it allowed me to glimpse something in her nature that was both celestial and subterranean. She was a unique creature, no doubt about it.

In the car, Xavier rambled on and on without stopping. He wanted me to run the lights. But I remained calm, shot through by that light your mother was emitting. I considered my friend a lucky man. Marriage is complicated. At the time, I still didn't know it. And it's true their marriage never suffered the slow wasting of days and years, from raising children. It almost didn't even suffer the contact of other humans. But somehow I got the feeling that beside Elenir, Xavier's life would be—I'm not sure what the word would be—simpler, perhaps, but certainly happier.

Life is so hard on us, in one way or another, that we end up transforming ourselves, inevitably, into beings that are smaller than the destiny that youth promises us. Xavier transformed himself into an addict—he became obsessed with anything that seemed to possess a new intensity: young girls, new authors, different languages, crazy ideas. A fool. It might have been different. Isabel married the already transformed

Xavier and for that she suffered, for herself and for her children. Long after Xavier's death, having witnessed your father's madness, I finally understood what kind of childhood and adolescence those kids must have had, constantly subjected to confusing and capricious expectations. I imagine that with Elenir he would have worked harder, been less frivolous. When she left him, the void that Xavier always felt, the one he'd tried to fill with devotion to his studies and his work—it only grew larger. In fact, it became a bottomless pit.

What happened was that he got scared, and I think that Elenir realized that it would happen again. Just by talking to you, I've been able to straighten out some things I didn't fully understand before. You told me that your mother was a doctor when she met your father, that she had her own house, and that he moved in. She'd glimpsed her destiny and then fulfilled it: all that was missing was a child born of a great love, a partner. You said that she refused to make use of the resources that Teodoro's parents could have offered, which would have minimized the risks her pregnancy posed. I did the math: she would have been forty-five when you were born. Let's suppose that she hadn't had any other children between Xavier's son and you, and that during the first Benjamim's birth her uterus had been damaged in some way, maybe due to the immaturity of her body or the primitive state of medicine in 1950—I don't know, maybe an aggressive use of forceps or a lack of adequate care after the birth. What I'm trying to say is that, since she was a doctor, she was certainly aware of the risks of having a child at that age, especially after that early and difficult birth. I knew Elenir, she wasn't prideful, that wasn't why she didn't ask for help. It would have been natural, after all, to appeal to the husband's family. She could have had the baby in São Paulo, in a hospital far better equipped to supervise a risky delivery.

You say she never met your father's family, that maybe she didn't know this possibility existed. That's a laugh. I only met your father after he got back form Minas, already eaten away by mental illness. His features were ugly and deformed, but even so it was impossible not to see he had Xavier's face. And even if he didn't, we have it inscribed on every millimeter of our skin, in our smells, the shape of our teeth, the way we say good morning and thank you—our birthplace and rearing. I have no doubt that Elenir knew exactly who she was dealing with. She might not have known that Teodoro was Xavier's son, the half brother of the little boy she lost. But she certainly knew he was from the same stock, cut from the same cloth. Yes, it was your father who didn't want help—he'd broken things off with his parents. Of course, Elenir would have known how to sail right over all that with tact—if that was what she wanted.

You mentioned religion, the mystic feeling your father had about forming a pure and new family: Catholic, but with Elenir's indigenous roots. But even you don't seem to believe this, especially now that you're going to have your own child. I'm right there with you: getting on with your life is a thousand times better than any of that philosophical nonsense. It's hard to believe that Elenir would have risked her life for some divine plans, or for the sake of marital isolation, or to defend a vague notion of a different and special purity. That madness of uniting love with isolation from the rest of the world—it wasn't something that came from Elenir, I assure you. Never. It definitely derived from the Kremz family. I also doubt that story he told you, from the time when she was pregnant, about how they spoke so calmly and with great spiritual elevation about the proximity of birth and death. Nonsense. You father was still a boy, he hadn't understood anything. I doubt Elenir even mentioned it. She knew all about the sterile agitation of men in those parts. I think it was her decision, and hers alone.

This luminous tale was later fabricated by your father, obviously, to help him cope with feelings of loss and guilt that there was something he could have done but didn't. I'm sure there's nothing he could have done. She was in control. She made the choice that suited her. We, men, are always played for the fools we are. Women do what they want, especially when it comes to family. I don't mean to say that Elenir wanted to die, but I know that after what happened with Xavier, the risk of dying was less painful to contemplate than the thought of becoming entangled with Teodoro's family. Even if she never worked out who this family was—which I doubt—she still knew its codes of conduct with respect to sons and heirs.

You need to remember that the person telling you all this is that boy Raul, a family friend who got scared and split right when his friend needed him the most. You know the saying: a man is only as good as his word. What I mean is, like any such add-on to a family, he drifted on to some new orbit as soon as things start going sour, and then he got to thinking he's independent, that he's someone who charts his own course. He imagines things, and he likes to play armchair psychologist. His aestheticized versions of things become his whole reality. He's just a pedantic chump.

Yesterday I went to visit Isabel in the hospital. I was in São Paulo, and thought I'd take advantage of the occasion to go see her. You're really getting into the old girl's head, distressing her. I know you don't realize what you're doing, and she'd never admit it to your face. And that's just the start of what she won't tell you. Oh, she's proud all right. Makes her independence a point of honor. She turns everything into a grandiose debate. That's why I told you that with Elenir, Xavier would have had a simpler, and most likely, a more productive life. Elenir wasn't one to defend her points of view, draw lines in the sand, or worry about the salvation of mankind or the fate of the nation. She understood people and she understood math, and that gave her a kind of impish strength.

I have to admit that our conversations are messing with my head, too. That's really why I went to see my friend Isabel. I didn't realize she was so ill. When we talk on the phone, of course she makes her terminal illness out to be just another bend in the road. Do you think it's right? That she's there all alone? Obviously she doesn't complain: it's not her nature to complain. But it's clear she's suffering. And aside from you and Renata, Leonor's daughter, none of her children or grandchildren ever come around. They call from time to time. Flora called when I was there, and Isabel was so haughty and dry with her on the phone that it makes you see why she'll die alone. Anyway, you should talk to your aunts and uncles, tell them to make an effort to break through the old girl's carapace and do their duty as her children. I mean really, what is this? She's become very bitter, I know how hard it can be, but goddamn, dying is hard, it'll be hard for them too, and she didn't exactly have an easy life. She raised four children, plus Xavier, by sheer force of will. It seems like the only one who goes to see her regularly is Leonor, but she'd just gone on tour when her mother's health took a turn for the worse. She spoke lovingly of you—a critical, bemused, and cruel love, of course, which for your grandmother is the highest category of love. She said she'd like to live to meet your son: she's been remembering things about Teodoro and Leonor when they were young, and it pains her that she can't remember certain important parts because she's ashamed of others. That's not something she'll tell you.

Xavier was disappointed at the directions that Henrique and Flora, his eldest children, chose for their lives. He started to think they were the mediocre ones. He put a lot of faith in Leonor's music, and in your father's more adventurous path. To maintain a sense of balance during their marital discussions, Isabel took the side of their older children—not least because they managed to start living on their own without needing money from their parents, and this was a great help to Isabel. It seemed like ever since they were little, Isabel felt she'd needed to protect Henrique and Flora from their father's ambiguous and exaggerated demands. With the younger ones, she believed the lifestyle and atmosphere she'd established in their household would be sufficient, and that there wouldn't be as much pressure.

Isabel remembers that Teodoro was always quite close to her. He liked to be near her, quietly drawing while she studied. His father's loud voice and heavy gait made the boy uncomfortable: he'd flinch when he heard his father approaching, and take his drawing somewhere else. This lack of any desire to please his father must have goaded Xavier into taking a greater interest, and the boy's dependence on maternal love afflicted Isabel.

I'm sure your grandmother didn't tell you about the two of us. When I met you, it was after you'd moved to São Paulo. By then the affair had already ended and I'd gone back to being just a close family friend—the only rich friend who remained, as Isabel says, with her peculiar acidity. The whole thing was really just a coincidence of timing and life events. After your grandfather died, I separated from my wife. Then I went through a period of diversion, taking advantage of the money I'd accumulated and whatever desire and vigor I still felt. After a while I felt a lack of camaraderie, of people who spoke my language, a lack of any possibilities of commitment. When I was younger I made passes at Isabel, but your grandfather was more captivating. By the time I got back from Paris they were already married. So anyway, fast-forward: things being what they were for each of us, I started coming around to see her. We went out to dinner a few times and saw some shows, but I realized that all she wanted from me was sex and distraction, no kind of commitment. I can see the humor in it now, but at the time it was pretty frustrating. The more I made myself available—even to help with her practical life affairs, like doing her accounting, which was already pretty tight, or helping her sell the last apartment building that remained from her mother-in-law's seemingly limitless real-estate empire, or helping her jump-start her kids' careers—the more I helped with all that, the more she saw me as just another man to take care of, and that was something she couldn't stand anymore.

We were wrapped up in all that for a year, until I convinced myself that it was impossible. I finally gave up. Nobody ever took care of Isabel—she was always the one in charge: first of her sick mother, then managing the house for her widower father, and finally her children and husband. I think that with Xavier, she thought she'd at least found a partner who could do his share of the chores. But that wasn't what happened. They shared love, ideas, and fights, but not chores. I could tell that she hadn't known about Xavier's regular episodes. What little she learned hit her pretty hard. Their pact was broken, the distribution of labor stopped being fair, Isabel began to feel like a governess to her husband and children—and being the family drill sergeant didn't please her one bit. Even though the role of the domineering mother never fit her, that was the persona she created for herself in their home, at the university, and in all the other work she did. She felt responsible for everyone. It was a feeling that weighed on her so heavily that she tried to liberate Xavier and her children from every single one of life's mundane obligations, to build them a space where their only obligation would be to grow up and be brilliant. She raised a bunch of irresponsible ingrates who are incapable of the most basic displays of solidarity, like visiting their dying mother. Isabel cultivated a true horror of responsibility in them, and at the same time overloaded them with the responsibility to be nothing but the best.

I wanted to marry Isabel. I wanted to take care of her, so powerful and so lacking. But she didn't have that kind of space in her life anymore. After a hard life, being cared for would have meant, for my friend, being imprisoned and suffocated. She couldn't see that what was suffocating her all throughout her life was the obligation to take care of others and receive nothing in return. It's strange, just think: for Fernanda, my ex-wife, caring for other people was also an obligation. But she liked it, so it was a fair trade: being cared for, and then caring for others. That feeling of being beholden to family was a delight for her, as well as an absolute necessity. Everyone had their role in the family and there was nothing more comforting to her than playing it well.

Isabel's disquiet always attracted me. She didn't realize that the only light shining from that house was her—and not any of the people she was killing herself to support. A light that maybe burned too bright, one that ended up singeing the floor where her protégés stood. Your father realized this early on—he managed to get away, but went to the other extreme. It didn't jibe with his Paulista blood, there was no way of fixing it. Maybe Elenir was capable of setting him straight, but she ended up doing to him the same as she'd done to Xavier.

She abandoned ship, digging the Kremz family hole a little deeper—that crater that I never really understood.

Women like Isabel were brought up to be one of a pair, to raise their children and make a respectable home. Then they were trained in school to build a new world. And precisely because they were women, they believed what they were taught, chasing these mutually antagonistic objectives. In the end they had to give up their independence and demand that their husbands and children accomplish the enormous ambitions they'd been forced to repress. Isabel had a respectable career, something few other women were capable of doing. She ended up a full professor at USP, and that still wasn't enough. She achieved institutional respect, left her mark on the history of the university, wrote a few books of literary criticism that, according to her, barely grazed the skin of the world, of this country, this city. It's a shame that in her final hours she hasn't managed to recognize her enormous worth.

Want to see your grandmother blow a gasket? Just give her a compliment. She'll shoot daggers from her eyes and start willing the earth to split open right under you. She's completely incapable of feeling like she deserves any kind of esteem, admiration, or help. She's lying there dying, and she continues to pontificate about ideology and literature, criticizing her children, her grandchildren, herself. Goddamn! It seems like even death is something she thinks she doesn't deserve. It's not easy for anyone, I know, but it's even harder for someone like her. My God, how humbling to be eaten away, slowly and constantly, death gnawing a little more every day.

Death for the first Benjamim was quite different. He was born weak. Elenir wasn't much of a talker—she communicated with her eyes and her hands. Throughout the martyrdom of her little boy, Elenir wouldn't leave his side for a minute. Xavier was terrified, called his father, summoned specialists. They wouldn't let her nurse him, they tried risky treatments. They hoped to recuperate the baby's brain functions after the damages caused by a clumsy use of forceps, procedures that ended up costing the poor little boy his life. Elenir wanted to save her son: she didn't care if it meant permanent brain damage. She tried to take him out of the hospital. She wanted him to continue his life or get on with his death—in her arms, against her breast, at home. It was a muddled state of affairs. We didn't know a thing about medicine, only that Dr. Kremz was a great doctor and that it would be irresponsible to disregard his advice. Xavier was firm with Elenir. He faced his fears with a feminine weakness and allowed his father to take charge. I still think the poor thing would have probably died either way. Elenir didn't make any accusations, but she felt betrayed by her husband, pushed aside. She thought the men cared more about the illness than the dying child.

Sometimes I sat with her in the waiting room at the hospital while Xavier conferred with his father and the other doctors about their son. Dona Silvia was always there, too. They treated Elenir like an impediment, attributing her revindications and her way of expressing her suffering as signs of her low breeding, befitting a person who didn't believe in science. There was no solidarity whatsoever, not even the Catholic veneer of it. I was young, I was close to that child, to my friends. I was distressed by that lack of empathy between Elenir and Xavier's family. I knew they were all wonderful people, and I knew that Elenir wasn't the threat that Dona Silvia and Dr. Kremz imagined her to be. But those were other times. There was no room to argue. Everyone took offense.

They attempted surgery and it didn't go well. Benjamim lay in agony for two days, still at the hospital. After that there was nothing else to be done. They transferred the baby to a room where Elenir could finally be with him. The room that had a sitting area adjacent to it. Dona Silvia received visits of condolence there, and prayed with a group of her friends. They were hoping for a miracle. They talked, got emotional. They spoke about the beauty and the bravery of that little angel, about the lengths his grandfather was going to save him, about Xavier's grief. They recounted other tales of parental afflictions, other sick children who were saved. They drank juice and coffee, and wiped their mouths with embroidered napkins, but without really wiping, lest they stain the napkins with lipstick, instead pressing lightly around the contour of their lips with a softness that's as forgotten today as those simple, delicate embroideries. They wiped their mouths, stretched their legs in the corridor, spoke in low voices, made sure not to clatter the china, and walked softly so their steps wouldn't be heard in the next room.

Dona Silvia accepted Xavier's orders: no one was to enter Benjamim's room, no one except his parents, the doctors, and me. But that isolation proved impossible, and the sound of the dishes, the prayers and conversations—it annoyed Xavier. He was exhausted. Occasionally I managed to drag him out of there to spend a few minutes drinking at a bar near the hospital. He wouldn't stay long before wanting to go back, only long enough to cry in silence over his drink. Elenir held the limp baby in her lap, connected to all those tubes. She massaged his little feet and hands, caressed his face, his closed eyes. Her fingers traced the contours of his ears, his thin neck. Her hands seemed to converse with her son's body as she said goodbye to him. They were beautiful hands, strong and brown, the fingers long and knotted. The image is engraved in my mind: that dark hand and the nearly transparent body of that little boy in the silence of that room. I got the impression that the child was being molded by those hands, and sometimes it even seemed like he was starting to show some color. It was just a trick of the eye—he was probably becoming cyanotic. The whole thing depressed me and I wished he would just finally die. Xavier had to force himself to go near. Elenir would take his hand and try to make him participate in that final conversation. She wanted Xavier to touch their son, feel the rhythm of the blood that still ran through his fine veins, hear the heartbeat with his hands. He couldn't do it.

Xavier couldn't stand the sight of his limp, dying son. He couldn't stand being away from Elenir, or being near her. He asked her to put the baby in the crib so she could rest for a while. She obeyed him and lay down on the small sofa in the room. When she tried to touch her husband, he'd recoil, choking back vomit, sobbing and breathing in deep huffs like a captive horse. I think she made him ashamed of himself, ashamed that he hadn't been able to save their son. He wouldn't look at the child. He seemed to feel nothing but hate and shame. He hated Elenir's caresses and the life that continued to exist in the sounds emanating from the next room. He became aggressive, started yelling at Elenir: leave the boy in peace, take your hands off him, the boy's already rotting, can't you see? Don't you smell it? A doctor who was in the room at the time called two strong nurses to hold Xavier down, because by that point it seemed like he might strike Elenir at any moment. They gave him a sedative injection. He fell into a deep sleep, I think it was even before the medicine could've taken effect. It was like he couldn't stand another second of any of it and managed to shut himself down. His circuit finally blew.

I went back the next morning. The boy died not long after. Elenir dressed her son in white and asked for the wake to be held at home. Xavier, dumbstruck, lay slack in an armchair, staring at the floor. Dr. Kremz spoke roughly to Elenir: "It's over. Can't you see my family has suffered enough? We're not going to draw out something that never should have happened in the first place. Enough. The body will go from here straight to the cemetery, today." Elenir faced his reproach, alone to withstand his harsh decree of bitter and final erasure—of herself and her son. When Dr. Kremz said the word "body," I saw Elenir tremble. She didn't cry or respond. Something inside her had broken. An even sadder tone twinkled darkly in her eyes, the sadness of having her heart ripped out. Her hands lightly clasped the little arm of her dead son, and something flowed between woman and boy, as though Elenir had swallowed her son's soul, protecting it in some hot, red-blooded place within her. Her body paled to the color of the dead boy's clothes. I went to her side, afraid the trembling meant that she might faint. Elenir took my arm and opened a different set of eyes than those she'd closed: tired, apathetic eyes.

She went to speak to Xavier, she wanted to go home with him, take a bath, get ready for the burial, escape from all those ladies and gentlemen who meant nothing to her or her son. Elenir knelt down and whispered to her husband. He didn't seem to hear her, or even recognize her. She smoothed his hair, caressed his face. She tried to make him get up. He didn't move. I said, "All right, Xavier, go home and get cleaned up. Elenir needs your help." He looked at me with fright, as though he didn't understand what language I was speaking. Dona Silvia, standing beside her son, said, "Haroldo, could you please take her? I'll take care of him. It'll be better that way. Can't you see he can barely get up? How could he help anyone else?"

Elenir caressed her husband one last time, kissed her dead

son's little hands, his eyes, murmuring in the child's ears a melody that seemed to emerge from her stomach. She made the sign of the cross on the boy's forehead and followed me out of the room without saying goodbye to anyone else.

Isabel

I let them give me morphine. It's gone now—I'm gone. But at least the pain is gone, too. I have to speak very softly so I don't irritate my throat. They say that it would be better if I didn't talk—they're threatening to take me to the ICU. But I had a chance to speak with Marcelo, my doctor and friend of many years, and he agreed with me. If I can't die at home, as I'd prefer, if life had turned out differently, I'd at least be able to tell whether it's day or night, without all these other deaths competing alongside mine. I'd be able to see your face, and remember Teodoro. What's the point of trying to save my vocal cords? Save them for what, the worms? Yes, I know what they're saying—don't believe it, and please, don't repeat that nonsense to me. It's over, that's the truth. There are no more second chances, no afterlife, no new drugs, no reason to save anything for later—that's all nonsense. It's over because this has become too much of a drag and I'm ready to throw in the towel.

Leonor called me from Paris yesterday afternoon, and called again today. She has her last concert tomorrow. She wants to cancel it and come home to see me—I think Renata must have given her a scare. I forbade her from doing that. It makes no sense. I told her that you and Renata were taking care of things. Are you staying in my apartment or at Leonor's house? At Leonor's, with Renata, that's what I thought. You always liked your cousin. She's a sweet girl, she'll be coming by here this afternoon, and maybe Henrique and Flora, too. Of course Haroldo has tried to meddle with my death, calling my kids and telling them to mind their filial duties—which is too bad, because family obligations were always what annoyed me most. I like to be alone. There's nothing charming about being seen by your children when you're so ugly and weak. With you and Renata it's different—I can tell that you both have a spirit that's more, more ... I don't know what to call it. There's a more complicated backstory between us.

Henrique and Flora are like Xavier: they're not good at confronting illness. Flora was overwhelmed. She'd cry, then calm down, and then make up a story to console herself, a story that fit illness and death into a moment in her life when "Everything was preparing her for this experience." For Flora, we always end up stronger and wiser and whatever. Even the flood of corruption in this country, the death of her brother, the failure of her little clothing boutique in Vila Madalena, her lack of gumption to continue with her acting career, her drug-addict son—all of it, in some way or another, is "preparation." Henrique is the practical type: he observes things scientifically, evaluates them, weighs the pros and cons. He believes in science and progress. He did exhaustive research on the Internet about this kind of cancer and its treatments. He knows the names of the medications, he talks to Marcelo—he's the reason I'm still here, hospitalized. He got really frustrated that we couldn't do the treatment in the United States, where I'd have access to newer drugs and better chances. The doctors that might help, friends of my father's—they're all dead, and I don't know anyone from the new generation, the ones who could pull some strings.

Henrique tried to talk to Haroldo, the last of us who still has money. I was so furious that it put him off the idea.

Henrique reminds me of my father—he became a systematic sort of person. He probably has a big planner where he makes note of all his commitments and the problems he needs to solve. Finding out how I'm doing seems to be an eleven-thirty commitment. Every day he calls me at exactly eleven-thirty in the morning and tells me what he thinks about all Marcelo's decisions. He tries to convince me that we're on the right path, that there's a reasonable chance we'll kick this thing. I don't argue with him. I'm grateful from the bottom of my heart for the effort he's put into lifting this burden off my shoulders—all the negotiations with the hospital bureaucracy, my insurance, listening to Marcelo and arguing with him. But the fact is that we're not in it together. Dying is intransitive. It's not something you can share. It's a singular subject, never compound. Even collective deaths, holocausts, gas chambers, massacres—they're still individual deaths. Everyone dies alone.

Henrique wastes a lot of time on me, I know that. I recognize it, and I'm comforted by his kind of care—you could even say his kind of love. But he doesn't come to visit me. For someone who believes in salvation and redemption, for someone whose optimism is a kind of moral obligation, a terminal patient is intolerable.

With Teodoro I saw this solitude of the very end quite clearly. Later I forgot about it and now I recall it again with the same clarity I had back then. When Dona Zefa called to tell me he was sick and in the hospital, I was sincerely grateful for her solidarity as a mother. He'd been hospitalized for fifteen days already and Dona Zefa figured it was something much worse than malaria. Some of the doctors back here in São Paulo speculated about insufficiently cured syphilis, which would explain his later insanity. Teodoro liked to think of that too: the madness of the greats. But he was my most beloved child, not one of history's great men, and the name of the illness made no difference. While he was in the hospital, Dona Zefa took you to live at the big house and treated you like a son, or a grandson, something that I found deeply moving. To this day it brings tears to my eyes to recall your total helplessness, both of you, and Dona Zefa's generosity. No matter how rightly we live, there's always going to be a moment in life when help is needed. I cry when I remember that sometimes there's someone there on the other side, ready to help. It does happen.

Your gentleness comes from there, from the goodness that you had the luck of finding there in Cipó. Just look: you went to the pharmacy and brought me two different kinds of reading glasses. You thought about me, you weren't sure which ones I'd like better. You don't really know me, or you know me so little, but you still thought about me. You see what I'm trying to tell you? It was something that came naturally: I complained about not being able to read anymore, you remembered, and you went to the pharmacy. It's something so simple, who wouldn't do that for someone in need? And that's how you see it.

I didn't end up using either of them. Even with new glasses I can't read. My ability to concentrate is totally shot. I get nauseated. I've been experiencing strong feelings—images, sounds, things I remember—I don't miss the printed letters, black and white, the way they jumble around. It's not a problem with my vision, it's a lack of desire. But you brought me two pairs of glasses.

I pictured you in the pharmacy, the clerk explaining the

difference between one model and the other while you tried to remember the shape of my face and the glasses I used to wear when you lived with me. Maybe an old scene came back to you: one of me putting on my reading glasses and trying to help you with your homework, reading a text along with you so that you could find the answers. And I pictured you in the pharmacy chuckling at the memory, of you saying, do you remember—"This glasses make you look like a grandma." And I told you, "*Those* glasses, Benjamim, it's not this glasses. Glasses is always plural, the plural of glass." At the pharmacy you probably smiled when you recalled me showing you the word "glass" in the dictionary, and in the end you didn't really remember exactly what they looked like, those glasses from that afternoon when I didn't hear you finally make the discovery that I was in fact your grandmother. There's something funny about it: what I heard was you telling me I was starting to look old, and on top of that I noticed the grammatical error. And the memory came quickly; it was funny and sad, and the image of those glasses I used back then didn't come along with it, so you decided to buy two pairs. That's the gentle sweetness I'm talking about. It did you well to grow up and get married far away from here. I'm certain your son will be a good and generous person. He'll know how to care for you when it's your turn to get old. If you want my opinion, you should stay in Rio, let Antonio grow up far from this complicated mess I made.

That was one thing I thought about after Teodoro died. I thought that if your father had stayed in Cipó, maybe he'd still be alive and well. I know that everything has changed quite a bit, and that there's no such thing as a simple place anymore, nowhere on the entire planet. But even so, I think the backlands are a more natural place for the nuts, the crazies, anyone who isn't quite right in the head. Because it's somewhere all the roles are more defined. Why is it that anomalies are less threatening in places like that? I don't really understand it, or maybe there was a time when I did—my head feels hollow, only stories interest me now, explanations are starting to seem too boring, too unreal. I once read an article about a study that explained nature's tendency toward diversity, especially in the tropical forests. In a limited area, there's a cycle that plays out between the rare and the common species of trees. When one type of tree becomes commonplace, individual trees start to die off, making the species more scarce. And the species that was rare starts to proliferate, and after a while it becomes commonplace, too. Scientists think that it has to do with distance from relatives. When there are too many close relatives nearby—consuming all the same nutrients, requiring the same quantity of light and water, sensitive to the same types of plagues—the species starts to diminish. But when you're the only one of your species within a certain area, the tendency is for you to grow stronger and reproduce more easily. In other words, to live long and well, stay away from your relatives. Be scarce.

Teo's problem, the one that led to his death, was the confluence of two factors: being crazy in a place where insanity isn't tolerated, and being too close to his relatives. Anyway, the two factors were really one—it's the relatives who can't tolerate insanity. Or maybe it's that the madman can't tolerate his condition with relatives hanging around. Or maybe it's that every family needs someone to play the role of the madman. After Xavier's death, the role fell to Teo, and he didn't know how to perform it with his father's savoir vivre, the quality that allowed him to take advantage of that character he played in his profession, in our family, and in the various beds he slept in.

It seems like the Germanic blood of the Kremz family skipped a generation, only to resurge with greater concentration in Leonor and Teodoro. That way of going hammer and tongs at everything, of never doing anything half-assed. Because she's a woman, Leonor was able to pace her passions. Your father not so much. I wonder if everything that came later, here in São Paulo, wasn't the product of syphilitic delirium. I don't think it was ever cured: he had constant headaches. Syphilis passes from person to person through intimate contact, the same as insanity, and I feared for myself and my family.

All that trash in my little apartment, the looks from the neighbors, my conscience. We've never talked about this, I don't know if you ever noticed how I dealt with your father's madness. I remember the first time I went into the room you shared—which I thought might still be able to serve as my office until I opened the door and saw that trash all over the floor and realized it would never be possible. Standing before that horrible confirmation of Teo's insanity, the feeling that came over me was one of injustice and revolt. I'd raised my children, watched my husband die, and finally had my own place—smaller than what I'd expected in my youth, but it was mine. I could afford it on my salary, it was conducive to my work, it satisfied my need to be alone and was fine for having company. And at that moment it looked like the trash from every house and every street in São Paulo and all over the world had been dumped in my house to destroy the space I'd worked so hard to create.

I opened the door and saw every single piece of the chaos in microscopic detail. Orange peels, cigarette butts, bits of metal and plastic, parts of electric appliances and broken furniture, shards of glass, pistachio shells, peanut shells, strands of twine, doll heads, arms, and legs, rusty cans, empty boxes and packages of every size and shape, nail clippings, clumps of hair, candle stumps, paper clips, old rubber bands, lumps of wax, clippings of photos and headlines from newspapers and magazines, old pictures of him and his two younger siblings, photos of my wedding, Xavier and I when we were young, linens and rags, tissues dappled with blood and snot and who knows what else, all of it arranged in a way that was similar to those cities he built as a boy. My books were stacked on the floor and the shelves had transformed into a repository of boxes in which he meticulously sorted his stock of human and urban detritus. There was a filthy notebook in which he made an accounting of each piece of refuse, crazy annotations about stock moving in and out, statistics. He planned out the whole project in an equally useless notebook. He said that here in São Paulo nobody worked, they only had projects, and so he was going to develop a project, too. Aside from this trash room, he began to form a crust of filth on his body. In the kitchen he made a flour paste to glue things together. There would be paste on his arms and face and in his hair for days, in addition to the dirt off the street, mixed with sweat and his own saliva. He spat on himself—it was a nervous tic he didn't even notice anymore. Yes, I know that you were there and witnessed all this. But I have to say it, I need to remember, I need to know.

You know, Benjamim, I forgot so many things just so I could keep going. So, so, so many things. And there was an infinity of things I never wanted to know. Now there's no-where else for me to go, there's nothing ahead, and the for-gotten things and the never-known things are what I think about. Every day I think more about him and his crisis. I'm like your father now: I need to vomit and spit for days at a time, and there's still more and it hurts and it stinks, a smell from inside. An interior odor, like the one I'd smell when I was menstruating. Not the smell of blood. It was something else, the smell of something that wasn't born and never will be, but still exists—the death of something that never came to be. I'd spray perfume, your father would get so filthy. I think it's the same thing, those strong odors.

After a while he started disappearing. He'd go several nights in a row without coming home. It pained you. I remember your soft steps through the apartment, in the early morning hours. I couldn't sleep, either, but I was wary of joining you, and having to talk about Teodoro. What could I say to a boy who was just eleven, twelve years old? You were a child, more childlike than the other boys your age in São Paulo, a joyful little boy without any malice and completely open to the world. In just a few months you matured and closed off. When I talked about your father with Leonor or Henrique, you'd run off to that room full of your father's trash and your grandmother's books. You were studying, or that's what you said. We tried psychoanalysis and medication. Teodoro would cooperate, then resist, and it was dangerous for him to be self-medicating like that. It was impossible to talk to him. He'd start to explain his project to me in words that made sense, using solid arguments and well-constructed sentences. But it was all empty. Nothing connected to reality, it was a dry well I got sucked into. His language was sharper than ever. He had the capacity for synthesis, depth, irony, originality, citation, fluency—everything in excess of truth and beauty.

He drew relationships between the material from which a fingernail is made and the material from trees that's used to make paper, and the process of creating the chemical element from silver that affixes the image of the person whose fingernail it is to the paper made from the bark of trees in the presence of sunlight and of the observer who snaps the photo. All of it was somehow united, in some way I don't remember, to the banter of bums on the street and the relationship between their speech and the headlines in the papers, on the radio and TV. The upshot was that the beggars' banter, because it was a random synthesis of the daily news, was capable of predicting future events. All this had to do with how beggars walk around barefoot and experience no interruptions to the flow of energy between the sun and the earth. The permanence of their ability to transmit an essential, organizing energy of human life, especially of the human gaze, combined with the beggar's rejection of the hollow, immediate flows of urban life: it allowed them to see into the future, the same way that people from the countryside can tell that it's about to rain, or can sense an earthquake—a beggar, who walks directly on the asphalt, which transmits information faster than the raw earth, is capable of predicting things like car accidents, the contents of a politician's speech, the results of an election, an assassination.

What else do I remember? Conversations I had with your father, things I heard him say, they come back to me now, mixed together. And I turn them over, searching through them, his endless monologues. They were as beautiful as he was, until the end. I know that Haroldo has a different opinion: that's one of his defects. Haroldo doesn't see things clearly. He lost perspective. Just look at the way he tells a story about the past: the images he retains are full of detail, his stories are enveloping because he's there, completely inhabiting the story he tells. Other times his sensibility carries him away on didactic digressions, defenses of the way he thinks the world should be. Whoever falls outside that order is deformed, ugly. Any delicacy of perception can only exist in those moments when his permanent defense of himself and his way of being in the world is temporarily suspended. That's the only time Haroldo can see what's right there in front of him. He gets scared, dumbstruck, angry. He finally feels with the other person's skin. Haroldo is one of the most intelligent men I ever met, but he's conservative. He never managed to understand the world I built with Xavier, our marriage—much less believe that we were happy. He only ever saw weakness and madness. At the same time, he was attracted to our radiance. But he wasn't capable of seeing the real Teodoro, the beauty of a delirious young man, a beauty that didn't derive from the delirium itself—that's only beautiful in novels—no, he wasn't capable of seeing the beauty of the young Teodoro, his eyes brimming and bright, his dark black wavy hair, his thin body, his way of walking and gesturing with his hands, like a thin stray cat, his fine and well-drawn mouth already half-blue. Haroldo could only see Teodoro's madness as something that was destroying me.

Yesterday I had a dream about Teodoro. I dreamt that what he told me made sense. I can't remember it exactly, it was a dream of forms and feelings, a perfect incandescent sphere that fluctuated in space and was absorbed by another, larger and less hot sphere, and so on, again and again. Inside the sphere was a violent and threatening motion, but it left the surface harmonious and smooth, like the breath of a sleeping baby.

Your father thought it was possible to decode the elements that make up the human soul, but that it was necessary first to define the concept of what he called the "soul of the planet." This soul was present in every interaction between men, as well as in every chemical reaction that could occur on or beneath the earth's crust. He said that art, especially music, deters mankind's ability to place its soul—humanity's soul—in contact with the soul of the planet and the universe, which in the end was a single soul. Art was a movement and not a thing, a movement of reunification and recognition for all those who were capable of seeing, hearing, feeling, and performing part of that movement. And for those who experienced the art, creating it or recreating it was in the act of looking, listening, or reading what was created. That is why, Teodoro told me, it doesn't make sense to talk about an unappreciated or unrecognized artist. An artist is only an artist when he's recognized. What makes him an artist is not his art, but recognition of his art, because it's the recognition of what he's created that generates movement.

I don't know if he told you about any of his theories, or if you'd remember if he did. When Teodoro resumed his wanderings, the sole of his foot started to look like a horse's hoof. In those days of dissolution, he'd shut himself up in that room to catalog his collection and organize his data and conclusions those notebooks. Did the two of you talk? I remember that on another night I wasn't able to sleep, I went to the kitchen for a glass of water and on the way I found you asleep on the living room sofa, in front of the muted television. The light to your room was on, which probably meant that Teodoro was in there writing and raving. Yes, that's right: he said whatever he was writing out loud. I'd forgotten about that. He'd let out a few disconnected words at a time, then he'd suddenly get very still, repeating the last word he'd said in various tones and rhythms until he was able to find his way back into the flow of his writing. I don't know how I could have forgotten that. Listening to your voice now, it's like I'm able to hear it again. Sometimes he'd write so fast that the words transformed into sounds, like he was playing a woodwind instrument. It really must have been impossible to sleep in the same room as him.

I remember our conversations about the things we needed at home and the little list we kept hanging on the door of the refrigerator. I remember how we divided up the chores, and how whenever I woke up the sofa would already be fixed up again, your bedsheets put away. And how in the afternoons, you'd wipe down the furniture with a rag to clear the grime left by the air pollution while your father's voice droned on in that room. I'd gotten used to eating out, or buying prepared food, usually pasta. After the two of you came back I had to teach myself to cook all over again. The day I decided to make steaks, your face lit up with so much excitement I almost cried. I hadn't realized it, but of course, you were an adolescent, going around half-starved with adolescent hunger. I considered taking a leave from the university so that I could care for the two of you. But I couldn't: Xavier's illness had liquidated our savings, including what we got from selling the house. And anyway, I knew I wouldn't be able to expose myself to Teodoro's madness for twenty-four hours a day. I needed that slice of sanity in my day.

It's true that you went to stay with Leonor for a while. Then she moved to Paris with her husband and kids so she could continue her studies. We even discussed the idea of sending you along with them—at least to give you six months away from all the chaos, and to give me a little breathing room. But we never talked to you about it. You were more attached to your father than ever before. During the days he stayed at home, you wouldn't leave, even if it meant skipping everything else. It must have comforted you, to some extent, just being there by his side.

I thought that maybe if he were away from me and his siblings, Teodoro would feel obliged to behave in a more civilized manner. During the period you went on vacation with Leonor and your cousin, Raul offered to take Teodoro for a while. There, at least, he'd have to take a bath and keep all his garbage in a suitcase with various internal compartments that he'd built and painted with the same whimsicality of those plastic monsters he used to put together as a boy. He'd be forced to have normal conversations with people. With Teodoro at Raul's and you on a trip with Leonor, I was able to sleep for six hours at a time, without being haunted by insomnia.

All the commotion meant that I finished my personal statement—the "intellectual autobiography" for my file at USP—in a way that was completely different from what I'd imagined when I started it. I was supposed to analyze my academic trajectory, commenting on each of my works to retrace the path I'd followed. This was so I could be considered for promotion to full professor. I remember it was June of 1991. Raul's wife, who was pregnant with their first child, was traveling with her parents when Teodoro went to stay at Raul's. The storm around me began to calm. Teodoro's project remained where it was: spread across the floor of my office and over some of the shelves. But its expansion was halted, and I was able to open up a path from the doorway to my desk.

I don't know which of us was the Palestinian and which the Jew in this story. If the idea is that a child will always possess a natural right to a piece of the motherland, then he was the Jew and I was the invading Palestinian. Not exactly me, but my work. My work had occupied the same space that was supposed to be reserved for my children, and later for my grandchildren and great-grandchildren. Obviously my status as a mother came before any other activity in my life, not least because there was no other way. But on the other hand, without my work I'd have turned into a crazy mother, saturnine: I'd have devoured my children one by one, or I'd have bossed them around so that they'd always, eternally, be children. Because the minute they stopped being children, I'd have no other justification for my own existence. Without my work, we couldn't have afforded the schools they attended. And that apartment they're fighting over now—it wouldn't even exist. There were some semesters when I chose my courses based on what my kids were taking. My writing was always more fragmented and meandering than what my male colleagues produced. Going over it all again like this, I started to see myself as the Jew seeking a reencounter with a prior state, one in which my future plans were clear and aligned with what was expected of intelligent, competent, and well-educated people—the life I'd glimpsed before my children were born, which I'd regained when Leonor married and left and finally the house belonged only to me. Teodoro's madness wore me down from every direction and the way I'd managed to defend myself was to attack him.

Taking a bath, chewing with your mouth closed, getting up early, figuring out college or some kind of work, helping you with your homework, going to parent-teacher meetings, getting you into some kind of English classes and sports, smiling at people and looking them in the eye when they said hello, cutting his nails, giving him pills at the right times, maintaining a shred of autonomy, trying not to lose my mind. All that was after he got out of the hospital, after they treated his illness. Apparently nothing worked and I had to accept that his fits of delirium had nothing to do with malaria or syphilis. It wasn't an act or laziness or some kind of lifestyle choice. It was madness, plain and simple, and I didn't know how to deal with it.

The first time he disappeared, I called a few of his old friends. But nobody knew anything. I didn't know if I should call the police, the hospitals. He was thirty years old. It was strange to be out all over the city searching for him. My innate sense of reality had broken down. I no longer knew what mechanisms I should activate to manage Teodoro. Was he a man or a baby? Was I to nurse him or force him out of the house? To what degree was he competent or incompetent? At first, Leonor thought that I needed to put food right into his mouth, get him dressed, fill the bathtub with lukewarm water and scrub the filth off him with a firm, careful hand. But there was no bathtub in the apartment and the big old house was no more. My breasts had long been dried of milk. Henrique thought that I had to draw a line in the sand, set boundaries, deliver an ultimatum: if you want to live here, these are the rules, the schedule, and the procedures that have to be followed.

Teodoro didn't react to any of these methods. The food was never to his liking and his random hunger didn't correspond to any schedule. He wouldn't bathe and slept with the bums in the street for two or three nights at a time. If I hadn't taken him in—well then, that's where he'd have ended up. And meanwhile, I needed to do my research, write, teach, and take care of both of you. I couldn't do any of it right. Teodoro slipping away, you wouldn't talk, and my intellectual biography was going nowhere.

While you were on that trip with Leonor and Teodoro was staying with Raul, I felt like I was in paradise. I didn't need a better solution—one solution, any solution, was enough. I shut myself in that office and wrote all day long. In twenty days I'd written more than three hundred pages. Almost all of it was garbage—just like everything that piled up around my desk. Cigarette butts, half a sandwich, cold pizza, dirty coffee cups, more cigarette butts, bunches of papers, open books, scribbled in, crossed out, note cards in all different colors, aspirin tablets, some pinga that I ended up drinking straight from the bottle. My trash mixed with Teodoro's and invaded the rest of the apartment. Piles of dirty dishes in the sink, rumpled clothes thrown on top of the unmade bed, bags of trash that I couldn't find the time to take out. I gave the housekeeper a month off and unplugged the phone. I didn't want any interruptions. It would just be me and my work.

During that month I let my body go. I didn't take a bath or brush my teeth or comb my hair. Nothing. I directed all my energy to writing, writing, writing. Almost without thinking—the words came from some other wavelength. Any external noise, music, my jaw popping—it concealed my thoughts and left my intelligence to my hands, letting them find the way. Somewhere in my body all that knowledge I'd constructed and stored over decades: it existed, I only needed to maintain a state of unimpeded, uninterrupted flow between that stockpile and my hands. I was overtaken by a trance and I finally understood what writers mean when they say they don't control their work. The trance didn't come from outside, it didn't feed into the writing. It's a noise that blocks thoughts of responsibility and sociality, brings forth some other quality of thought, and sets it in motion. My face flushed. At the end of a page that I thought to be particularly brilliant, I'd moan with pleasure, howl with delight. I'd put on loud music and dance around the apartment by myself. In my final hours of work, which usually happened around dawn, I'd have cramps in both hands and an intolerable headache. My stomach would start to remind me that I had a body. Time for bed, time for pinga.

What pulled me out that trance that was morphing into a madness bent on destroying my body and my home, what pulled me back out of myself and my insane pleasure, and thrust me back into the reasonable flux between life and work, back to a purer pleasure, sincere and elevated—it was my lower parts. Defecation and sex. A clogged toilet and the desire for a man. Laugh, Benjamim, and don't look so uncomfortable. You can think of it as my senility and not the truth. I never told anyone this. I don't like to talk about sex. Everything is already so sexualized in this country, so much tits and ass, so much vulgarity, that I ended up a prude. I blush. Do you even know what that is? Does it still happen? It used to be that young ladies would blush whenever the conversation alighted on any carnal aspect of life. It seemed back then like nobody ever went to the bathroom. Sex was simply nonexistent as topic of conversation over lunch or dinner. Well, I kept on blushing. In our house, Xavier would force the issue. We talked about everything, and anything having to do with the human body had always attracted him. Whenever the conversation went in that direction and the snickering started, I'd get up from the table, go fix dessert, help Graça with the coffee. Sex is an important subject—no, it's not a subject, it's an important thing. It's hot and sublime. So why dilute it in public, why this chafing of words, libido rising into the saliva and ears of those at the dinner table? Could it be that they don't understand that words are solid things, and not just channels, ships, boxes? People think that words bear meanings, images, and histories from here to there and there to here—don't they see that words are hands, knives, hearts? I never liked talking about sex, hearing about sex, or seeing sex, but I always liked having sex.

With Xavier it was good. He knew all my spots and liked to make me happy. After his illness and death, I was so exhausted that my body didn't demand it. A year or two later, desire returned, and I didn't know what to do with it. Xavier was my first boyfriend and I'd already forgotten what to do, how to act. As a woman over fifty, I was no longer naturally desirable. Some kind of effort would be necessary. The thought of it shamed and even offended me. I had a few flings, they were fine, but nothing special. To be honest it was good but weird— weird to be with someone in just this one way, and then they're gone. Something separate from the rest of the day, like going out to dinner. But the few things that did happen reactivated a desire that didn't fade. That was when Haroldo reappeared. We had a nice time together. With him the weird part was the other way around: he wanted to be mixed into my days.

I'd already had a sufficient dose of being a wife with Xavier. I didn't need any more of that. When the two of you came back to São Paulo, about four months before that crazy July, I realized that I didn't want any man by my side, trying to give me advice, meddling with my life. It was too much static. I had to take care of my kids? All right. And keep working? Fine. And take care of the house? Okay. But a boyfriend on top of that? No, that was too much. Haroldo said I had to learn to leave more time for myself and not always go watch my grandchildren whenever my kids asked me to, or run off to help out whenever one of them hurt themselves, or agree to be on so many thesis committees and still participate in all the department meetings and torture myself trying to pre-pare a lecture that was as good as those I'd given in previous years—or this, that, or the other thing. I'd laugh. I laughed be-cause this so-called time for myself was really, in the end, sup-posed to be time I'd spend with him, listening to his side of the conversation, going to the movies together when I didn't really feel like it, just because we'd already made a date with friends. It meant helping him buy clothes, taking a marvel-ous trip over a holiday break when there were so many other important things to be done, like sleeping, reading, thinking, and sitting around doing nothing. It was impossible to be idle, just reading a book or watching a dumb TV show, beside a man as active and organized as he is. I need moments of tedium throughout my day. I need sit and stare into space for hours, my eyes glazed like a dead fish. It's a way of maintaining homeostasis in my organism: alternating continuous activity with moments of hibernation—novels and crossword puzzles, for example. With Xavier I almost couldn't manage it, and with Haroldo it was even worse. Things were already going badly when I decided to go to Minas to rescue the two of you. We had a more serious argument than the ones that came before. We thought it was best for each of us to go our own way, and I never thought about it again. After you got here, after Teodoro's madness invaded my life, I never had a chance to miss him.

Burrowed into my Dionysian, narcissistic, masturbatory month of writing, dancing, drinking, writing and writing, garbage and more garbage, piling up in every corner—in the middle of all that, the toilet clogged. It was my salvation. Something had to be done—and I tried something myself, but it didn't work. For two days I used the sink, but it couldn't go on like that. It was a throbbing sign of the degradation I'd allowed myself to fall into. It started to smell bad. The only thing left to do was call the plumber, but to do that I had to put the apartment back in order, clean myself up. You can't just open the door and let a stranger into your house looking like that, even if he's only the plumber. I had to take off the nightgown I'd been wearing for days, take a bath, make the bed, wash the dishes, open the windows. In the bathroom, bleach and Pine-Sol. In the kitchen, Ajax for the porcelain, detergent for the dishes, the feather duster and the vacuum for the bedrooms and living room. I aired out the pillows and comforters, I flew clean sheets on the clothesline, filling them with fresh air before I put them back on the mattress, which I'd cleaned with a brush dipped in alcohol. Dirty laundry went to the washing machine, then the dryer. I ironed everything. Straightening and cleaning, I started to feel bad about not having done it every day. Not because of the way it made the house feel, but for the way it cleaned out my head. Working with my hands, distracted, would have been a form of meditation, a pause during which ideas could shift around, letting the good ones remain while the bad ones sink down, or float up and out the window, borne away on the fresh breeze blowing through the apartment and on the wings of my song. A housecleaning like that would have done me good—many housecleanings throughout those happy, lonesome days. Just to ease my mind, straightening and mumbling or singing old sambas at the top of my lungs: "Barracão de Zinco," "Ave Maria No Morro," sambas in which the poor are a figure of speech, like the American drifter and the Irish fool—that primordial and universal human misery, all of us and our shared solitude, my crazy son, my helpless grandson, all of us.

The deal I'd made with your father was that I'd keep his trash city intact, and only clear the routes I needed to move around. In my mania of cleaning and straightening and drying and putting things way, I threw all that trash away and felt immense relief. I cut my fingernails, washed my hair, rubbed the pumice stone on the soles of my feet and used a rough rag on my knees and elbows, stripping away the old, dead skin. I massaged my entire body with creams and dabbed perfume on my neck, behind my ears, and wrists.

With the windows open to the sun and breeze and smelling delicious myself, I called the plumber and asked him to come by. He was a happy, handsome boy. We talked while he worked. He started joking around, so did I, the kettle boiled, the house filled with the smell of coffee. I was completely drained. During the previous twenty days I hadn't eaten or slept well, and after cleaning the house and my body I was completely exhausted. My arms hurt, my heart was light, and my head was swimming. I loved being able to talk to someone again, watching the body of man as he worked, laughing at the dirty jokes he told me and laughing again the ones I told back. He was taking apart the pipes with a monkey wrench, putting screws in the holes and lubricating the grooves, getting the water flowing again, letting it run for a while, telling me all kinds of silly things. So then, after everything was done and we'd had our coffee, it happened. Forgive me, but Mother Mary, it was so good. He was sweet and gentle, he told me how much and I happily paid. Then he left. I slept for hours and hours, I slept like the reasonable woman I'd go back to being, I was sure of it.

I woke up famished, with the notion that I could start anew, start at the beginning and do everything right. I realized that I'd behaved my entire life like a king, a strong and just king, a Chinese king from the I Ching, who doesn't invite anyone to adore him—everyone comes by their own initiative. The dependency of his subjects is voluntary. None of them have to repress themselves, they can express their opinions openly. Policing isn't necessary. Everyone, by their own free will, shows their devotion. This principle of freedom was valid for life in general. I never implored my children or any man to love me. I never understood any language that wasn't well-spoken Portuguese. The king is solicitous with those who seek him. He welcomes them, takes them in, shelters and helps those who speak the courtly language. Madness was never the courtly language, neither cries nor screams, except the cries and screams of babies. It was all wrong, primordially wrong. I couldn't court anyone, I couldn't grab my crazy, filthy son and cover him with kisses, I couldn't pay for sex. I couldn't because a king should never implore the favor of his subjects.

But now, I thought, it would all be different. The house and I were both clean. Son, mother, work, home, and body—it's all one single thing. We separate time into hours, a home into rooms, the day into obligations, and it's all just an abstraction. In fact everything is one. If one person is sick, everyone is sick. We're always the whole and that doesn't stop anyone from moving ahead, working, loving, caring. If the toilet clogs, the world stops, that's how it is. If you and Teodoro needed me, it wouldn't have done any good to shove it off onto other people and tell myself it was what I had to do for my career. Things don't work that way. I decided to call Raul and see how they were doing.

Things were terrible, and Raul was outraged. He'd tried to call me, he didn't know what else to do. Carmem had come back from her vacation and she couldn't stand the disorder surrounding Teodoro. The baby was about to be born, Teodoro was still doing his vanishing act, reappearing disguised as a bum, right down to his very soul, a bum who asks for nothing and needs everything: a bath, a meal, affection, enough! Enough, Isabel! I won't be responsible anymore!

He was mad at me and at himself. Furious. He thought he'd be capable, Carmem had the answers—it was just a question of space, of creating an atmosphere without unnecessary pressures and judgments. But the atmosphere was modified by Teodoro and assumed the features of his madness. The house went mad. Carmem was crying, locked in her bedroom, covering her ears with a pillow. Teodoro would disappear and come back silent and hollow-eyed. He didn't listen to music anymore, didn't play his guitar, didn't talk, didn't bring trash home. He was nearly mute. "And that's even worse, Isabel, I don't know what to do"—Raul talked at me without stopping, a torrent of resentment and frustration. I had to go and get Teodoro right away.

Teodoro was sitting on the sofa like a shamed child, tidy and sitting up straight. Raul invited me in for a coffee. Carmem didn't make an appearance. Teo wanted to leave. We went home in silence. I'd taken my work out of the room and fixed up a desk in the living room. I'd thrown out the little cushion you'd been sleeping on and bought another bed. I made the bedroom back into a bedroom. Too late. After two days of watching TV nonstop, Teo had a breakdown and we had to commit him. When you got back from the trip with Leonor, your father was already in the clinic, the shards of glass were in the trash, I'd had new windows installed, and the apartment no longer had a television.

I'm tired, Benjamim. I'm not in pain, it's just this sickness. Maybe that's what it's already taken from me, I don't know—it's a tiredness that isn't bad, just strange. After the rains, your father came home tired. He came from the favela, where he'd gone to live. I had a friend who lived there, he took pity on me. After the flood he brought me Teo, drenched and sick. We went straight to the hospital. He was burning with fever. You clung to him, the last friend your father had, listening to the story of his final deeds. He knew that Teo was dying: his story already sounded like it was passing into legend. We listened and couldn't recognize the skinny Teo who lay dying in the ICU. "Teodoro was a hulk, carrying children and furniture across the water in his arms. Everything fit in those arms, the entire whole world. The water was like a fire, it was just as dangerous and strong as a fire, tongues that licked inside and knocked everything over. He came and went from the shacks and saved a lot of people. His face and body were covered in mud—not even a fireman gets that dirty from the ashes of a burning building. And even after that he didn't sleep. He worked night and day to rebuild the shacks, without stopping to rest, day and night, working and getting food for the kids." You asked him to tell us more, to reanimate that nearly pulseless corpse that you wished you could still recognize. And he went on, talking about the furniture floating around, the falling walls, roof tiles flying, a small child crying on top a table that had become a raft. After that he went away. You looked at me, we looked at each other—do you remember, Benjamim? I realized that you were with me—we both knew that the Teo who had done all that was not my son and not your father. That saintly effort was undertaken by three hundred, three hundred and fifty Teodoros, and none of them was ours. Our Teodoro, frail and tired, was dying.

I don't want to talk anymore, Benjamim. Today the poor thing is me. A sick dog, a run-over cat, a bird that's flown into glass. Dirty and poor. My bedsores stink. My voice already sounds like a hoarse toad. Don't start telling me how much you love me, Benjamim, it's not the time for that. Nonsense. Go now, I want to sleep.

Raul

Having a child is one of the most radical things that can happen to you. You can live a thousand years and your life will never pass through another transformation as absolute as the one you're about to go through now, when your son is born. You have no idea. There are terms to designate a person's civil status: there's bachelor, married, widow, mother, and father. But there should be a word for the opposite of orphan—what I mean is there should be one term for people who don't have kids and another one for people whose children have died. I don't have the guts to visit Isabel in the hospital.

She has a dead son. It's the same present-tense verb that Teodoro found strange whenever your grandfather said: I have five kids but one of them died. Because I saw what happened to Isabel. Her dead son is present, maybe even growing old, because in the end his presence has followed his mother and brother and sisters into their later years. It's not his death that's present, it's him: the way he talked, the way he moved, his seat at the table. With a dead friend, it's the same thing. That's why I can imagine what it's like to have a child die. No, you can't even imagine it. Rafael is fifteen now, and Estela is twelve. I can't imagine it.

Time flies, it's true—life goes on, and a lot of things have happened that he was not a part of. He was already gone when my son was born, when I twisted my foot, when I took another trip with Carmem and he wasn't there to receive—or not receive—my postcards. And it's true that when when a person dies they disappear and their place becomes occupied by other people. Another friend will receive my postcard, or my desire to write postcards will be what fades—I no longer need him to tell me I'm being ridiculous. At the same time, he's still there, saying the same things, and there's still the street where his house was, the building where the school was, the São Paulo Museum of Art, the films we used to see together, which I now rewatch by myself. And you: you have his voice and his mannerisms. Isabel in the hospital, dying. I don't have the guts to visit her.

I kicked your father out of my house. You realize what that means? The fifteen, sixteen years that have gone by haven't undone that. The expulsion still exists, it always will, forever—like his sodden, wet death. I'll never be able not to have turned him out of my house at the time he needed me the most. Life puts itself back together, I know I don't have total control over something that was impossible for me to do: there was a broader context, and I wasn't the only one on the scene at that exact moment. But the fact is that I can't stop being the protagonist of my own life. I won't say that I did the wrong thing, or that I could have done something different. I don't know about that. Every day creates a different set of possibilities from what came before, and from what might have been. I know that I thought there were two options and that they were mutually exclusive: to fight for Teodoro, or for my son who was about to be born. I distanced my son from your father's madness and its destruction.

Today I don't know if what I felt was really a threat, or just my rage and Carmem's hysteria. Or, at least, an enormous laziness when faced with dealing with your father's madness. The way I feel rage and laziness about Rafael's adolescence—his banal revolts, the shouting, the loud music, his man scent spreading throughout the house, the infinite selfishness, his rude way of speaking to Carmem and the way she puts up with it.

You'll see when your time comes—you even get a little bit nostalgic and envious and even proud of the strength he develops. A territorial dispute. You'll see how it is. You were getting to that point and your father couldn't face it, because it's really complicated. With me and him, the thing is that I took the easy way out. I don't just mean that I didn't help him out—I was the one who showed him the door. The way things were with me right then, if I hadn't kicked him out I would've gone insane right along with him. Or I'd have figured out a way to kill him. Which is basically what ended up happening.

He was spreading throughout the house, constantly wanting to talk. He couldn't stop talking about his crazy theories. He wanted my opinions, my company. I'd tell him to go take a bath and he'd get offended, lock himself in the room I fixed up for him, the one that was going to be the baby's room, and start rehearsing all his crazy writings out loud, pacing from one side of the room to the other. It tormented me when the sound of his voice and footsteps suddenly ceased.

He'd leave and come back after spending time on the street, his face and arms cut up, his body covered in bruises. He was clearly starting fights, or getting caught up in them. I think he was cutting himself, too. One night I couldn't stand it anymore and went out after him. I found him, completely wasted on the sidewalk. I'd decided not to worry and not to go out looking for him again. But I couldn't sleep, thinking about the way he wandered around alleyways like a stray dog. I started going out hunting for him, bringing him home, tearing off his filthy clothes, running a cold shower and yelling at him to wash himself with soap, shampoo his dirty hair. He liked being treated that way, scornful of my despair. We were like a couple of fags. That's what he wanted, for someone to be his daddy, his mommy, his nagging little wife with a rolling pin in hand waiting for him to come home in the wee hours, or out combing the dirty city alleys at night to find him.

At first it even gave me some kind of pleasure, a feeling of omnipotence: I'll fix this guy no matter how fucked-up he is—I'll be able to bring him back. I bought some big ashtrays and placed them around the house so that he wouldn't spit on himself or all over the floor. In the intervals between his fits of madness, there were days of calm. They weren't exactly happy days—it felt like the type of exhaustion a marathon runner might feel after a full day of training. There were hours, usually in the early evening, when we'd order a pizza and sit together watching TV without the sound, just shooting the shit. We talked about stuff from our adolescence and childhood. He'd play his guitar.

We talked about Vanda and the stories she used to tell us while she made our lunch in the kitchen, the white cake on top the fridge, the bike rides and long walks along the banks of the Pinheiros River, the times we went to Casa dos Bandeirantes, Isabel's long speeches, the time Henrique fucked up his knee, blood all over the place and not a single adult in the house, about our model city and the parquet floor, tabletop soccer, plastic monsters, *Mad* magazine, *Get Smart* and *Bewitched*, *Bonanza* and Batman, his perverse drawings and stories, the unapproachable girls at our school, Terço concerts and the theater in the basement of that church on Cardeal Arcoverde, our friends playing the festival down in the Vila, nights at cafés in Bixiga, and early morning hours in the frozen streets of

São Paulo. About Xavier's theater pieces, the garage at the big house, the *choro* rock band that he formed and his big tape recorder, Flora's projects, that timeless tradition of exposed breasts in Brazilian theater, going out with Henrique, the sidewalks full of pretty girls, and how we'd spend eight hours straight watching movies during the film festival at the São Paulo Museum of Art, drooling over Norwegian films without subtitles, our discovery of Cortázar and Dalton Trevisan, our desire to have fun and make a difference and not know where any of it would take us—and his move to Minas.

In those early evenings, the wise and cool drifter, the no-mad who knew nothing of that world of the cheerful, willing slaves and cowards of frivolous urban joys—that persona was dormant. So was the backlands ranch hand who rolled his own straw cigarettes, took care of his little boy, and threw meal to the hens. All these mythic characters slept deeply and allowed us to talk.

Our past, the way we spent those years of adolescence: they were the great things that I held onto with care, things I liked to think about, things that helped me maintain the vitality we used to feel. For Teo it seemed to be different. Those TV shows, Jorge Mautner, movies at the museum, Muhammad Ali—he spoke about all that in a heroic tone. It was a big deal, a moment in time when our hearts were opened, a time that would never again exist in the history of the world, a time that was special for all humanity, and that we were lucky to be a part of it—something we had to try to resume.

There was no disdain or negation. Our childhood and adolescence weren't some kind of mistake. He wanted to recuperate the freshness that had remained there—or the tension, or the feeling of infinite time, our whole lives ahead of us. We were able to screw up and laugh about it, and dedicate ourselves obsessively to useless things without feeling any guilt or ambition. Without having a single obligation—no filial or paternal duties. As though it was all just a question of alignment, and then we could be back on that wavelength.

He'd tell me that you were a kid who had his head on straight, that you were strong, handsome, cool, and self-sufficient. He said he didn't have anything else to give you, staying close wouldn't do you any good. Anything he said or did would be a father's sayings and doings, something huge, a thousand times bigger than what it was to be just some guy saying this or doing that—which isn't much. And that you were going to want to obey him or disobey him, care for him or be cared for by him, get scared he would to die, or be ashamed of things he did. And he wanted nothing to do with any of that—he wanted to find his way and for you to find yours. That's what he was thinking when you were just eleven years old. You weren't even an adolescent yet, and he was putting distance between the two of you. He said that he couldn't carry you around anymore, and that you, at eleven, didn't need his stories and you weren't like the other little boys who asked for their parents' blessing on their forehead and then went and did whatever they felt like doing. He said it was his fault you were different, because he'd taught you that you had to lead with asking for whatever it was you wanted, without deceit or hypocrisy, without arguing or fighting, and to do what you thought was right and not do what you thought was wrong—wrong for you, for your conscience. He spoke with a pride he didn't want to have. He was tired.

"I raised him the same as they raised us, Raul, I set Benjamim at odds with the word rather than at odds with the world inside him. I took my time and did it calmly. I did it wrong, I failed at what was most important to me—I failed to achieve Leninha's calm. I never had it in me. I thought I'd figured out that way of being, or that I'd managed to cultivate in myself and in him that ability to see things without prejudice, without bringing a fight, just seeing and listening and then thinking. Having eyes and ears come first, and touch, too. Feeling the humidity of the day, the strands of each blade of grass. Do you remember Jequitinhonha? I was training myself and it went well, I thought I'd managed. But no. No—that nothing's not for me. So all right, since that's how it is, that's how it'll be. Benjamim will go his way and I'll go mine. He's strong, he'll be able better off with my mother, with Leonor, with anyone who knows all the things I already forgot better than I do. Right now I want to recover it however I can, that crazy way my skin split open and I understood everything with my mind. I want that mad desire."

He brought young girls to the house, really young ones. One girl this day, another girl the next. Neo-hippie girls, fifteen, sixteen years old. To be honest, they were all half-damaged—kind of like he was in those days. He put on a show for them. His memory was still phenomenal. He talked about music, bands from the seventies and eighties, about our friends who became pop stars—and their eyes would just glaze over. He always told the same stories, with the same details. He'd laugh and get excited at exactly the same sentence and he'd still sound sincere. He didn't do it out of some kind of calculation, it was something half-demented, like he was still an adolescent. It was stupid.

The street, the banged-up bums, the girls, the binges, the spun-out conversation, his insane theories, the filth and the loud music—I was completely fed up. I never knew how to approach him, or if he was going to respond like a child or an adolescent or a guy our age. At the time I was about thirty. And he manipulated me from inside his madness, played me for a fool. He asked me to loan him money, he'd take my clothes and wear them without asking, all in this childish way that didn't make any sense. I'd forget that he was insane and sometimes thought I was the one going crazy. I couldn't take it anymore, but I kept it up because I had it in my head that this was my duty, because I didn't understand there was no way to help him. Every day he got more reckless and raving, and my dedicated efforts only made it all worse. It further adulterated his perception of reality.

When she came back, Carmem, my brilliant wife, a perfectly sensible psychoanalyst, a woman who explained to me who I am and the things I do—well, that woman came back and went ballistic. She wasn't supposed to get back until the middle of July: she'd gone to spend the month with her parents at their house in Campos do Jordão. I stayed behind, working. That's why I told Isabel I could keep Teo for a month. But Carmem was pregnant, needy—she couldn't stand being away from me, away from the doctor. She wanted to start setting up the baby's crib. Anyway, the shit hit the fan.

She called one night, telling me she was coming home the next morning. In those days I had a regular gig at an ad agency. I had an important meeting and couldn't be here when she got home. Teo hadn't been home, either: he'd slept somewhere else. I tidied up his room, put all that junk he had spread all over the place into his suitcase and left early for work. But when Carmem got home she found a trail of vomit through the house, Teo blasting music in his room, and she almost collided with some girl who was dancing naked in the kitchen. I only got the full picture of what happened days later. When I got back to the house it was already one in the afternoon. The maid had already cleaned everything up, the girl was gone, Teo was sleeping, and Carmem was crying in our bedroom. She managed to blurt out something about having to move out, that she couldn't have our child there. She said something about the ghosts of madness and deprivation that would remain burrowed in the walls of the boy's room—the kind of things your father might have said in those days. Fluids, waves, spirits, and all the rest of that infernal nonsense. Two nuts under the same roof, with me in the middle. It wasn't viable: one of them had to get out, and fast. It was horrible to see Carmem like that.

I decided that Teo would have to go that same day, but I couldn't get in touch with Isabel. I thought she must have been out of town. She hadn't called even once—which wasn't necessarily bad, but now it was time for him to go home, and that meant going back to Isabel's. Leonor was traveling and I couldn't just kick him out on the street. So the three of us lived together another few days. Carmem held it together. She didn't speak to Teo directly and avoided crossing paths with him. He could tell the climate had shifted. He stopped spitting and kept himself clean. He got really quiet, took on a permanent air of guilt, and started slinking in and out of the house again, staying out for a long time and coming back still clean and quieter than ever. He was like a big dog who hurts his owner without meaning to, and then shrinks away from his owner's blows, practically dragging himself along the floor. It was a knife to my heart to see Teo like that, worse than seeing him manic and filthy. He didn't go meet up with the vagrants and the hippie girls anymore. Instead he'd go and sit on the sidewalk two blocks over, quietly, just sitting there the whole day without moving, doing nothing. On my way back from work I saw him on the sidewalk and only then realized that he'd been spending his entire day there, for several days in a row. I parked the car and sat down next to him. It was our last conversation before he was committed.

He told me that he stayed there because if he started wandering around, he'd get dirty and sweaty and his smell would make Carmem uncomfortable. So it was better to sit there in the shade—that way he didn't run the risk of hurting her any more. "I need to get my sense of smell back to how it was, so that I know when my scent is too strong. I need to be able to gauge the level of my voice, and I don't know if that will ever be possible." We went to a bakery nearby. He was starving. Ever since Carmem got back, he didn't eat at home with us anymore. He'd say he ate out. But he didn't have any money. He barely had any clothes. He'd given what little he'd brought with him to his friends in the street. I was worried about Carmem and feeling like I got conned by Isabel. But I couldn't stop thinking about your father's hunger, his guilt. He inhaled three cheese sandwiches and a glass of water. He said that prosciutto, mortadella, and salami had smells that lasted longer than cheese, and that he wasn't going to drink booze anymore. Just thinking about beer made him sick to his stomach. "I want to get to be a man without a scent, without voice, without volume." Even without wanting to, he seemed like he still had a lot he needed to say, right up until he disappeared. Softly and slowly, he said:

"Sitting there on the sidewalk these last few days, sitting still and eating nothing—it was good. I remembered some strange things. From when I was little, six years old, a vision from behind the slats of the fence at the empty school, watching people and cars and dogs going by in the street. My mother's friend's driver used to come pick up her kids and their friends, including me. He packed twelve kids into his van and went around dropping them off at their houses. One day he forgot me and I got left behind at school. My mother always told this story, but I'd never been able to remember it myself, with my own memory. My mother said she was panicked when everyone else got home and she realized I was missing. She went to the school and saw me with my little face pressed to the fence and could never forget my laughter when I saw her, a laugh that made her heart beat even faster. I liked to hear her tell that story, imagining my little six-year-old child's face behind the fence, watching for my mother. I liked thinking about the feeling of salvation I must have felt when I recognized her legs approaching.

"On the sidewalk, alone, in the shade of a flowering ipê tree, the actual memory came back to me. The empty school, just Conceição and me. She was sweeping the patio, the whole place, the two of us there alone. I went up and down the steps, into the classrooms, opening drawers and closets. I went into the principal's office and sat in her chair. I hung from the crossbeam of the soccer goal, then stood at the fence, looking through the bars the street. A sort of magic had come over the world, making it seem completely different. I knew something almost no one else knew. I was the master of that secret and I didn't know what to do with it.

"I saw the empty school. I saw it all out of time: the street the school was on, expecting nothing. I saw Conceição sweeping the floor of the school like it was a house, any old house that continued to exist without people in it. Discovering that things remain the same without our presence was something stupendous. I saw my mother's legs on the other side of the fence. And seeing the legs of a woman that turned out to be my mother, lifting my eyes to see her worried face—it was good to know that my mother was part of that parallel world, a woman. We went home in her car. She was wearing beautiful, colorful clothing: a short skirt, with her hair done. Maybe she'd just come from a luncheon. They weren't the kind of clothes she'd wear to teach at the university. She was wearing lipstick, guiding the car home. And sometimes she'd turn to smile at me in the backseat, reaching back to squeeze my leg.

"Riding home with her, we traced the same route as every other day—except this time in her Beetle, just the two of us, and she was wearing a perfume that she usually only used at night. The same route, rendered completely different by all these changes, different in schedule, right down to the hunger I felt, which became a confirmation of my new understanding of the world.

"Things were what we saw, as well as the other things that might be surprised if you could apprehend them in the moments they let themselves to be seen. Weed, alcohol, and that very different life in Minas, the physical exertion and immersion in a language and thought process that weren't mine—it all made me think that this was another state of feeling that anyone could experience if they were exposed to something different from their daily routine. It wasn't a feature of the world, but a feature of the human perception of it. But now, here in the street, sitting here on this sidewalk, I realize that's not it at all.

"These days I've spent under this ipê, sitting on a sidewalk covered in yellow flowers, I realized it wasn't just that. With these flowers, this hunger, this silence, right here on a regular sidewalk, there's nothing special about it, the same hunger and the sense of the commonplace, like the school when I was six years old. I realized that what I experienced in the schoolyard on that day and later, at other times—it's not only a difference of perception. The building, the empty school in this case, is completely different when it's full—not only in the way we see it, but the thing itself: the bricks, the color of the walls, the acoustics in the various rooms. I'm still there, inside: I hear my footsteps, and from the height of my little boy's eyes I see the shapes of the posters, I see the color of the walls with my chestnut eyes, and it's the same school and I'm the same boy I was in that moment.

"People want to have control over these alterations, at least over the material that remains stable between each different gaze. I think I went looking for that—here, and then in the *sertão*, in the mountains, in the streets, in animals, in death, in my son, in the poor. I wrote stories and composed music. I liked writing and composing, but was embarrassed by the pretense of doing it, the pretense of art in general. I still listen, in my memory, to the stories Vanda told us. She, that black mass who would sit on the edge of my bed when Leonor and I were still little, the two of us huddled together so that we could withstand the fear that Vanda could conjure with her voice. I remember her words, her pauses, and when I wrote and composed it was the rhythm of her speech that enveloped me and carried me away. My stories, poems, and songs came from Vanda, from the Bible, from Mr. Nestor, from Zezé in Catingueira, from Brinco, from Fátima Giló, from the earth of São Paulo, from Jequitinhonha, from Cipó, from the dust of any old street. My words and songs came from there, but they weren't anonymous, and they didn't belong to the clay under anyone else's feet. They were mine and I was ashamed of it.

"I never wrote about what happened to me: my biography, my chronicle, my philosophy. None of that ever interested me. I wanted to create something new and unique. I want nothing else."

I know I didn't kill Teo. There's no one to blame, not even him. I yelled at Isabel, I kicked him out of my house. He just sat there on that sofa, waiting for his mother to come get him. He left quietly. After our conversation at the bakery, he stopped talking. He went completely mute. He wouldn't even talk to Isabel when she arrived, smiling and pleasant. He got up and gave me a pat on the back, a gesture that seemed intended to give me strength in life, as though he was saying: you made it through a bad patch but now everything will be better. Buck up.

After he left, after I kicked him out, two or three days later he smashed everything in your grandmother's house. He smashed the TV, the picture frames, and he cut himself while smashing the windows. He'd calmed down by the time I got there. He and Isabel were both tired. Henrique was furiously setting things back in order, outraged by Isabel's inaction. I supported her. I agreed that Teodoro was the one who should decide whether or not he should be committed. I washed Teodoro's arms and wrapped his slashed wrists in clean gauze. I was relieved he hadn't done anything like that back at my house. I remembered him sitting on the sidewalk, clean, as well as drunk and filthy in the gutter. I thought it would be best if he were committed, or if he died. But he had to choose. He had to speak one more time. And he refused to say anything.

Haroldo came and called an ambulance. They put Teo in a straitjacket. It was unnecessary: he was completely calm. But nobody said anything. Isabel watched quietly. I looked away. A straitjacket with rings and buckles on a guy who was already weary and wounded. The straitjacket and Haroldo's authoritarianism were the same sort of violence as the broken glass in the apartment: proportional forces, perhaps, but the violence of disorder was the kind I understood.

The next day I went with your grandmother to the clinic. She and Teodoro didn't know what to say to each other. Or there was nothing left to say.

Haroldo

So now they're coming around. It's true, she wanted it that way: alone. And they believed it. It was comfortable to believe. There's no use getting worked up over it. It's finished. Now everybody's coming. At least no one can say it's for the inheritance. If anything remains, it's debt.

The last breath is a strange sound, like the thunder of the Twin Towers collapsing: the precise moment when something ceases to exist. The exact word for it is expiration: the last air to exit the lungs.

I was afraid that Flora would want to hold a wake for Isabel at home—that she'd put that burden on us, too. The first Benjamim is buried in the Consolação cemetery. By one of life's ironic twists, he's in the same tomb as those grandparents who never wanted him, far from his father. Isabel decided to bury Xavier in that bare, charmless cemetery in Morumbi. Maybe she wasn't so keen on being buried beside her in-laws. It was always her idea to separate, isolate, create a new family, a new man, without the stain of the past and the ancient things that come before us.

Xavier had the same obsession and passed it on to your father. Sometimes I see them as two demagogues, one abandoned by his people, the other devoured by them. Reinventors of the world who left only a void. Their method of isolation was establishing themselves in the midst of other people, laying their heads to rest in foreign places, wading into places other than their own. Your father went too far and too fast.

Let's go downstairs and have a coffee in the bakery. Leonor is nervous. It's better not to stay here. We have some time until the viewing starts. We should have a drink, we have the whole day and all night to hold the wake.

I had a crazy thought, one of those tricks the mind plays. I remembered that your father wasn't at Xavier's burial, and realized that now he won't be at his mother's. For the second time, he'll be the only one missing. I was already mentally upbraiding him for it, forgetting that he's dead. We've spoken so much about Teodoro over the past few days that somehow he's become more alive for me than the other three. I was a close witness to his death. I know he was just a confused young man who'd had his fair share of suffering. But even so, I can't forgive him for what he did to Isabel.

He was her son, but he was also an adult—a man. And my friend was a widowed woman. It doesn't matter that she was his mother. I'm talking about relationships between men and women, the young and the old.

I tried to defend my friend against the fury of a man who'd lost control. Unlike your great-grandmother, Dona Silvia, Isabel didn't have a husband to rely on, and didn't know how to preserve her sanity, or her world, from your father's madness. Probably because her world, and maybe our world, was nowhere near as organized as Dona Silvia's. Or because today, nobody is able to see the order that sustains it. In those days we knew what we wanted to reform and what we wanted to destroy. And today, what is there to maintain? What order is left to defend? The order of work, yes, of course, and maybe at least the natural order of things, as well, the one in which a man doesn't attack a woman.

I'm not here to play the ostrich, like Dona Silvia, and say that Teodoro's madness was just a spasm. He didn't know what he was doing. He was a sick man. But I also know that neither Isabel, nor anyone else in that family, had the discernment necessary to see that there's a world, and an order to it, and that our history must be preserved—that we're not just made of guilt to pay, with every outburst of madness in our sons, every attack from a poor man. Xavier and Isabel, with their need to feel open to everything, and their determination to expose themselves to every risk—that desire to live dangerously, on the edge of the abyss—they thought they were immune from the destruction of madness and misery. Or they supposed that madness and misery didn't necessarily possess the power to destroy whatever lay in their path. They were so special and superior that they could let themselves play at being poor and crazy.

Xavier and Teodoro, through eroticism, adrenaline, or boredom, opted for contact with the lower classes. But Xavier still had the apparatus of theater between himself and the workers. In the world we grew up in, the lower classes worked hard. They were the kitchen staff, factory workers—they made enough money for the bus. Or they lived in far-flung corners of the country: bumpkins, Indians, cowboys. Stories of the sea, the droughts. I used to go with Xavier to his grandparents' estate. We'd trek deep the woods and onto the plains with the cowboys, we went dancing at the cantina and came back reinvigorated. We got close to everything, to better recognize our country and the truths of simple people, popular culture, the salt of the earth. But it wasn't our truth. It wasn't an explanation of our history or our world. We inched toward the virile and primitive adventures of horseback gallops, cachaça around the bonfire, virgin girls. Then we returned to civilization. Not Xavier: he wanted to forget who he was supposed to be, he wanted a more profound transformation, he wanted the absolute truth. They, the simple men, they never forgot who Xavier was. That's why he came out of it alive and strong, full of new energy.

With Teodoro the motives might have been the same. They probably were. And anyway, to be honest, they're the motives for almost everything we do in life. The common people in Teodoro's day were the immiserated, the favela dwellers, the landless people, the homeless: people with no history and plenty of rage. They could never stop knowing who Teodoro was, and for that reason he came out of it weakened, almost dead.

Your father's madness radicalized a desire that he already possessed, one that might have been with him since birth— the same desire that took him to Minas. What I mean to say is that maybe even if he hadn't gone mad, the arc of his life and the tragedy of his death would have been the same. He didn't just need to come into contact with the earth of our land. He wanted to become it. The estates had all been dismantled, the lands the family kept were urbanized, a mudslide that destroys and sweeps away, to nowhere. It was there, in that nowhere, that he wanted to live. That was where he fled and where he chose to die.

I committed him twice. I took responsibility for it. Twice he escaped. The first time was when Isabel called me to help contain one of his outbursts. She was terrified by the noise of the windows and everything breaking, by the force of your father's rage. When I got there the doorman was trying to restrain Teodoro. The two of us managed to get a hold of him and pin him to the floor, still yelling and arguing. I had to slug him. Then he shut up and went limp.

Henrique came over to look after him while I went to look for the best place to commit him. I had to convince Isabel that it was the only option, that it was the best thing for him. In the middle of it, that Raul shows up and says he's there to support Isabel, telling me that only Teodoro can decide whether or not he can be committed. What an idiot.

I felt like punching him, too. If Isabel weren't there, that's exactly what I would have done. And not for lack of control, but by strength of conviction. He hadn't been there to see the state she was in, trembling all over. He hadn't seen the terror of her realization that her son might kill himself—and what she hadn't confessed, but what was obvious—the possibility that he might kill her, too. Couldn't he see that she wasn't in a condition to think clearly? Coming around like that to corroborate her indecision and guilt—and what was that all about, that indecision? An insistence on some kind of error, digging a little deeper into the hole where that belief in their omnipotence had thrown them, where it had thrown Teodoro. Demanding that he to take up the obligation of his own freedom, the duty of sanity. Henrique brought his mother closer to seeing the light. He showed her that committing Teodoro was the only way to help him recover the ability to decide things for himself. He knew how to talk to her using her own terminology. And Isabel accepted it, she agreed to commit her son.

The second time he escaped the clinic was by jumping out a second-story window and cutting himself all over. I thought that was really it—there was nothing else we could do. Maybe Isabel was sure of it, too. It was his choice, the path he had chosen a long time ago, the first time he left home. That first time he'd been saved by Elenir, your mother. There would be no one else like her on your father's path. The only other person to free him from himself, from his thirst for the abyss, was you. A baby, a son, is always such a phenomenal joy that it fills any man with the willpower to live. But Elenir died and you grew up.

We didn't know where he'd gone after his second escape, and I thought we should stop looking for him. If the clinics were unable to restrain him—that is, if he had the wits and initiative to escape—then I figured he'd be able to fend for himself. Isabel didn't share that opinion. One minute she'd still be thinking that he was the one who had to decide, that he deserved his freedom, including the freedom to die and all that. But when it came down to letting go, she couldn't do it. She'd get anxious, call the hospitals, go out looking for him in the street. An old friend of her family's, a priest, managed to find him in a favela. He'd built a shack on the edge of the Pinheiros River and was giving classes to illiterate adults.

I never saw him again, not before he was taken to the hospital where he died. He'd been in that contaminated water for hours, and since he was already so weak he'd picked up some kind of aggressive infection. He wanted to cure himself with teas and herbs. I think he wanted to die right there in the favela. During her visits there, Isabel befriended a neighbor, someone much more sensible than your father. This neighbor promised her he'd keep tabs on Teodoro, and he was the one who finally brought him to the hospital.

I don't know what they told you. I remember you were always there in the apartment, shut in your room, studying. I don't think you went with your grandmother those few times she ventured into the favela. She took notebooks, pens, and pencils to Teodoro's students. She also brought him volumes of pedagogy for teaching adults to read. She tried to collaborate, to support her son—until she realized her mistake. "He doesn't want to be a good teacher. He isn't concerned about how well they read or write. I think he's resolved to become some kind of saint. He helps people fix up their shacks, he teaches them how to do things, and he says they know some things that he needs to learn. He talks about being generous with the children and paying attention to what they say. He speaks indignantly about the violent things he's witnessed, tales of abuse that he's heard people tell. He's become an intolerant person. He has no interest in anything outside the favela and steers clear of anyone who isn't like him, like them. He barely eats, sleeps very little, rainwater leaks onto his bed. He won't fix his own shack and he's gotten very thin. I'm not going there anymore. He doesn't want me to come, and I don't want to be there. He knows that he can come home whenever he wants. He wants to teach people to think with their own heads. But where's his head been? Where's that restless intelligence? He teaches what he doesn't know, he tries to extract something from them that they don't even have. And they're so hungry, all of them, hungry for everything, for the things Teo could teach them, to read and write. Teodoro is hungry for their hunger. Their hunger is the most important thing they have. It's what saves them, he says, his dedication will help them understand that they're competent people, lovable people, because he loves them. But I'm of the opinion that they don't need him to know that. I think they need him so they can learn how to read and write. This good Teodoro is the incarnation of an older man who always existed, an empty and universal space that people enter into, and feel good."

I started getting together with Isabel again. There was no romance or anything, even though she was always the woman of my life—even during the reign of Xavier the Insane. She pretended not to believe it, but she was flattered by what she called my "jest." I can't say it's true that I always loved her. For many years I never thought about her. But every time I saw her, I started thinking about how lucky Xavier was, and how foolish she was to have married him and not me.

I never managed to get close to her heart. I couldn't understand her soul. I wanted to defend her from herself, shelter her fragility. And it was only in her final days, when she was on the brink of death and still fighting, that I finally understood. She didn't want to rest, and that might have been the only thing I had to offer. She didn't want to arrive at any destination: she didn't want to win and didn't want to lose. And I understood nothing. And if I had understood, what then? Would I have given up? I know I wouldn't have. And now that she's dead, I'm more sure of it than ever. I loved her and now it's over. The possibility is over, the impossibility is over. Everything's over. I always knew how to be the provider, the problem solver, able to discern a system in the chaos, decide on objectives and devise a strategy. Maybe that was why I felt so drawn to Isabel. She was my particular chaos to domesticate, the girl from a good family whom I used to walk home. She had no home to return to.

Preparation of the Body

Isabel died at six o'clock on a São Paulo evening in her green room at the Severo Pinto Hospital, founded by her late father-in-law. At four o'clock she'd fallen into a coma. Her children and grandchildren were notified. At five-thirty they were all gathered around her. Half an hour later, her heart stopped beating. Her grandson Benjamim and daughter Leonor were with her for her final lucid moments. Leonor came straight from the airport. Renata dropped her mother at the hospital and went to work. No one knew that it would be Isabel's last day. She had persistently rejected all previous prognoses and proved them all wrong. After she started taking the morphine, her resistance yielded, and she could no longer struggle against death.

Leonor entered the room with bags under her eyes, not having slept on the plane. "How was the concert?" Isabel asked, suddenly, without so much as a hello—she wished to avoid pleasantries, and banish the fright in her daughter's eyes—fright at the sight of her wounded, cadaveric state. "How was the concert? A standing ovation in Paris?" Leonor laughed, the panic melting from her face. She kissed the dry skin on her mother's sunken face and responded playfully, "Oui, maman, pas mal, vraiment pas mal." Isabel closed her eyes. The worst had passed. Once more she'd taken the initiative. It wouldn't be so bad to end her life with a question. She'd done well. Until the very end, she'd done well. *Pas mal.* She closed her eyes and passed away. Her body tarried for a few more hours before it followed.

Flora started crying and went with her daughter Laura and another friend, a florist, to make arrangements for the viewing. Henrique clenched his fists and his eyes, unclenched his fists, opened his eyes, and approached his mother's body. He gave her a delicate kiss on the forehead, straightened a few strands of her hair, caressed her still-warm face, and went with his son to the cemetery to have the tomb prepared. He was in the middle of the corridor when he turned back, opened the door to his mother's room, and without coming in, asked Leonor, "You think she still has that silk shirt with the different colored waves? I think she'd have liked to be buried in that." He went down the corridor with his son, said hello to Dr. Marcelo, his mother's friend and physician. They traded a few condolences before each went on his way. Although he knew the noise would bother sick patients and although he was, in his day-to-day life, a discreet person, he let his feet fall heavy on the tiles. The loud sound of each shoe striking the floor and echoing down the hallway helped to calm the scattered beating of his heart.

Henrique started the car, buckled his seat belt, and sat still, holding the steering wheel with both hands. He wore a slightly old blue blazer and a white shirt, open at the collar. His knotted tie was in the jacket pocket. Beside him, his son wore a light gray overcoat with a modern cut, and a maroon tie pattered with bright orange diamonds. Grandma Isabel would certainly not have approved of this playful aesthetic joke of combining a very 1960s orange with a classically dull maroon. It might even be supposed that Fábio had chosen exactly that tie to emphasize his cheerful capitalism to his tyrannical grandmother, never mind her moribund state. It could easily have happened that way, but today he hadn't thought of his grandmother. As he put on his tie that morning, Fábio had been thinking about the pink-haired girl from the marketing department.

Fábio buckled his seat belt and turned to look at his immobile father, dazed at the wheel, oblivious that he'd just started the engine, that it was time to put the car in reverse, back out of the spot, and get going. Fábio wanted to say something. He was moved at his father's state. He couldn't think of anything to say about his grandmother, about the death that so saddened his father.

"She never liked me," was what he came up with.

Henrique laughed, threw the car in reverse, backed out of the spot, and shifted into first. He handed their parking validation slip to the attendant at the booth and continued on toward the cemetery.

"It's true. Not that it means much."

They continued for a few minutes in silence. São Paulo was sunny and cold, the streets as packed as always. Inside the car, Henrique and Fábio wore their jackets. It was a workday, quitting time, everyone heading home. And the two of them, father and son, were on the way to the cemetery together, in one of those suspensions of time so precious to Teodoro, in which the quotidian world becomes strange. São Paulo, streets and cars, the beginning of spring, a girl crossing the street, Isabel no longer existing. Inside that bubble in time, an *entretemps* before their mother's and grandmother's death consolidated as fact in their lives, Fábio said things he hadn't realized were important to him.

"I didn't love her anymore. I think I did when I was little, but it's been a long time since I've loved her.

"And you're your grandmother's grandson. That tremendous vanity and sincerity, the delicacy of an elephant tramping across the room, boom, boom, boom."

Henrique got quiet. He wasn't angry—Fábio knew that. But it was better not to go on. Henrique had no sense of direction. If the conversation continued, they'd be more likely to get lost than if he remained silent and focused.

A friend of Flora's had brought exotic flowers with excessively sweet fragrance. Laura came in carrying three vases, which she'd borrowed from the hospital staff. She stopped and sniffed, like a distrustful dog. Her skin was brown, like her grandmother's. Her body was gym-toned and naturally curvy. Laura helped prepare the room for her grandmother's wake, her belly sticking out, a deep neckline exposing her beautiful breasts. Around her neck she wore a small crucifix on a gold chain. Flora, who'd mostly collected herself, got emotional seeing her daughter standing in the middle of that room, so beautiful and exuberant, so contrary to death. Laura put the vases on a table and, making a childish face, objected:

"The smell is overpowering, it's going to make everyone dizzy."

The florist replied with feigned nonchalance, irritating Flora by seeming to take pleasure in shocking them: "The smell of the body will only get worse, which is why you have to have strong flowers. The two smells mix together and people think it's just the flowers. It's less disturbing that way."

Flora took Laura outside to collect yellow flowers and lilac blossoms from the sidewalk under the tipuanas and the jacarandas lining the street. It embarrassed her daughter. As much as she loved her mother and understood what she was going through, she found it a bit much to be crouching down on the sidewalk in front of the hospital to gather up dingy flower petals. She discreetly sat on a low wall, lit a cigarette, and looked the other way. Crouched against the ground, paying no mind to the clamor of buses and cars going by, belching exhaust, Flora continued her sad and distracted collection, remembering a time when the world was full of expected things and everything seemed possible, the days when her mother would come and wake her in the morning hours when she had rehearsals. It had been a long time since her path in life parted from her mother's, and in that hour it was all too painful to recall.

In the hospital room, Leonor and Renata, assisted by two nurses, washed Isabel's body. The nude body was tremendously ugly, as was the brusque way the two nurses roughly handled a woman who was, after all, the two women's mother and grandmother. Leonor sent Renata to her grandmother's apartment to look for the wavy multicolored shirt from the sixties, back when they were all kids and their mother was beautiful. It would be sort of like a costume, Leonor thought, a costume of the youth and the joy that left her mother's life so long ago. But Henrique's right: the burial is for us, and not for her. We can choose the mother to whom we say goodbye.

Still wearing the clothes she'd put on when she left Paris, almost the same outfit she was wearing when she'd received the applause after her concert—*pas mal, maman, pas mal*—Leonor, without any further explanation, asked the nurses to leave her alone with her mother and the cleaning supplies.

"Remember: you have to be quick. From this point on, the body will stiffen and then you won't be able to get any clothes on her at all, not without tearing them or breaking her bones."

The two of them left the room, the fat one saying over her shoulder: "The cotton balls are important. You don't need to know why. Just believe me, dear: put them in every single hole."

Leonor forced open the stubborn windows of the hospital room. She wet a towel, dabbed it with a drop of the eau de cologne that Isabel kept by the bedside, and began to clean and perfume her mother. She turned the torso slightly and saw the sores and purple bruises on various parts of her delicate dry skin, in places where her mother's body supported its weight in bed. To turn the body over, so she could clean her mother's back with both hands, without having to use one of them to hold the weight of the body, she had to turn Isabel completely onto her side, so that her whole body was resting on one arm. Although her mother was thin and light, it was still a body with arms, legs, and bones—something difficult to maneuver while inert. The lack of weight made things more difficult rather than easier.

Leonor forced herself to forget that the body was her mother's when she forced it onto its side, pulled one arm underneath, and bent the top leg, propping it on the bed to support some of the body weight. She regretted having dismissed the nurses. She ran the perfumed towel lightly over her Isabel's back, avoiding the sores because she thought the cologne might sting. There's no one there to hurt, she reminded herself, it's just a body. A chill went down her spine and her legs felt woozy, but she continued, cleaning the wounds with the perfumed towel. She turned the body back over. Then she leaned over her mother's body, rubbing perfume on her wrists, behind her ears, on the nape of her neck. Leonor's silver necklace with African seeds got snagged in her mother's thin hair.

"Sorry, mom, just a second, I'll get it out without hurting you. Hold still, I'll get it out."

As she untangled the necklace from her mother's hair, she began to cry tears of rage and confusion. She managed to separate herself from her mother's body, and stood looking at her necklace, still with a few strands of her mother's hair attached. A horror rose in her throat. She ran to the bathroom, splashed cold water on her face, and took several deep breaths.

She went back into the room and covered Isabel's body, including her face, with a sheet. She remembered it was a cold day and put a comforter on top, still confusing the line between life and death. She sorted some of her mother's belongings left strewn about the room: eau de cologne, hand cream, a book, a slipper, a hairbrush. Toothbrush, newspapers, cookies left by visitors—this kind of thing went in the trash. At the sound of gasses exiting her mother's body, Leonor trembled, frightened, then continued straightening up.

Renata returned with her grandmother's clothes. After they got her slacks on, Renata slowly lifted her grandmother's back so that Leonor could fasten her mother's bra and slip the shirt around the other arm. The silk short-sleeve, with thick multicolor waves. As they lifted and twisted the still-limp body, what liquid remained inside it flowed out in a brown stream.

"Shit, shit! The fucking cotton balls—that's why!" Leonor screamed in rage.

The stench filled the room and the bodies of the three women. Startled, Renata let go of Isabel, causing her body to slouch into an odd position on the filthy mattress, an arrangement of the neck and shoulder that would be impossible for a living body. She only glimpsed her grandmother's neck in that strange position—she didn't even hear the bones in her neck crack. She ran to the bathroom, ripped off her clothes and turned on the shower.

Leonor removed her soiled shirt and straightened her

mother's body. She fixed the angle of the head and closed her mouth by tying a handkerchief around her jaw. Slowly and carefully she balled up the dirty sheet and the plastic lining underneath, as carefully as if she were handling a baby. The mattress hadn't been soiled thanks to the lining. She used a wet towel to clean the filth off her mother's face, neck, and shoulders, then used a dry towel and finally the perfumed cloth. All cleaned up again, and now she won't roast under that blanket, Leonor thought, laughing at the deliberate confusion, she'll be able to sleep nicely.

She took the silk shirt to the bathroom to clean the soiled collar and sleeve in the little bathroom sink, and ended up washing her clothes along with Renata's, which were still on the floor. Nothing that soap and water can't take care of. In the shower, Renata was scrubbing her entire body to be rid of the smell of death and hospital room that had clung to her in these last weeks, impregnating her body day by day. She scrubbed with soap and cried from rage and fatigue. Leonor took off the rest of her clothes and got into the shower with her daughter. Slowly the two embraced, and each cleaned the other's body.

Benjamim bid farewell to Haroldo and crossed the street in the direction of the hospital, getting hit by fat drops from yet another October shower. The city would be flooded again. Some people would lose their homes and others would be stranded in traffic. A thick night had fallen by the time Benjamim, tired and sopping wet, entered his grandmother's hospital room. The room was already empty. A hard rain was coming in the window that someone, distracted, had forgotten to shut.